# PRAISE FOR *SMOKE HOLE*

'When I started reading *Smoke Hole*, I noticed the hair on my body growing faster. Midway, my fingernails needed to be clipped sooner. By the end, my voice had dipped from a Barry Gibb falsetto to a Barry White baritone. If you dare ... read with care.'

— **John Densmore**, The Doors;
*New York Times* bestselling author of *The Seekers*

'Through feral tales and poetic exegesis, Martin Shaw makes you re-see the world, as a place of adventure and of initiation, as perfect home and as perfectly other. What a gift.'

— **David Keenan**, author of *Xstabeth*

'I read this book in one sitting. It was impossible not to. Enthralled by the first story, much as I might have been enthralled at face value by a childhood fairy tale, I read on.

'Every now and then a book comes along which turns your world view inside out, and upside down. This is such a book — at once beautiful, enchanting, compelling, disarming, sobering — but ultimately liberating and enabling. Martin Shaw is a powerful storyteller, and what a story (of our times) he has to tell. We would do well to listen.'

— **Brigit Strawbridge Howard**,
author of *Dancing with Bees*

'"The mess out there is because of a mess in here." With this, the fundamental teaching of all true paths, Martin Shaw launches into his great theme: what the wild, and the myths it gives birth to, can tell us about this baffling, broken moment. There is no way out without a return: maybe here you could find a story that will rescue you.'

— **Paul Kingsnorth**, author of *Alexandria*

'A beautiful, quietly radical book. Shaw opens the world of ancient mythology and applies it to modern life, offering the reader a poetic olive branch to help reconnect with – and, crucially, re-enchant – the fabric of life itself.'

— **Harry Sword**, author of *Monolithic Undertow*

'In *Smoke Hole*, Martin Shaw magnificently demonstrates how we need old stories to guide us through the very modern perils we are all now facing, from the pandemic to social media. His storytelling and use of language are dazzling, and through the prism of entrancingly poetic and vital tales of challenges and great testing, he illuminates the power, comfort and absolute necessity of the old stories. This is an important book: thought-provoking, heart-healing and life-enhancing; showing us how myths and metaphor can reconnect us to the wild, help us rediscover a sense of awe and find startling beauty in the strangest and most terrifying of times. Stories are always for those at a crossroads, says Martin Shaw, and as we all find ourselves at a monumental crossroads now, we need to look back to the old stories and let them show us the way forward. Martin Shaw enables us to see how if only we can learn, once again, to listen to the vital teachings and old-world wisdom held within ancient stories, they can, quite literally, save our lives. This is a book with a deep magic and a crucial message for our troubled times. To read it is to be taken on an enriching journey, to gain a new perspective, or maybe an old one. I absolutely loved it.'

— **Fiona Mountain**, author of *The Keeper of Songs*

'Ontological dynamite. Cutting through the techno-utopian verbiage of our age, Martin Shaw's husbandry – his appreciation and respect for the power of modern tools; his awareness of their limits and dangers; and his instinctive reverence for the timeless, the essential and the vital – will awaken the tamed metaphysicist itching to run wild, who sleeps in even the doggedest technologist. A rare kind of modern-day bard, he walks a tight rope, guiding us to that very special place where we can learn to be wiser, worthier, more generous ancestors without failing to show ourselves to be more humble, sensible and compassionate descendants.'

— **Felix Marquardt**, author of *The New Nomads*

'In language as resonant as his human voice, master myth-sayer Martin Shaw summons us away from our frantic distractions to that wild place where the answers arise, crows in their hair. *Smoke Hole* gives us the sight to recognize them. Seize this book. It will be the deepest and most delightful reading you do this year.'

— **Sarah Chayes**, author of
*Everybody Knows* and *The Potomac River*

'Is it possible for a small book to contain the vast wild? Can its pages hold the cool breeze, the rustle of small things, the secret history of the earth and of your own face? Can a book help to break the spells holding us prisoner? *This book can.* Our time is one of breaking and breaking open, and Martin Shaw's tales help us to reimagine our world so that we can rebuild on the ruins of our untenable civilization.

'Martin Shaw is that rare teacher whose soul is a harp string strung between the urgency of heartbreak and the joyful ferocity of hope. The music he makes is deeply moving and challenging in the best of ways. The stories and lyrical teachings you will read in *Smoke Hole* help guide us to a more ethical, a more lucid future.'

— **Ariel Burger**, author of *Witness*

# PRAISE FOR MARTIN SHAW

'With potent, lyrical language and a profound knowledge of storytelling, Shaw encourages and illuminates the mythic in our own lives. He is a modern-day bard.'

— **Madeline Miller**, author of *Circe*

'His work combines a magnificence of soul with an acuity of intellect … he writes in the rare register of an earthy seer and I am in awe.'

— **Jay Griffiths**, author of *Kith*

'A consummate mythteller.'

— **Bill Plotkin**, author of *Wild Mind*

'A true master. One of the very greatest storytellers we have.'

— **Robert Bly**, author of *Iron John*

'Piratical brilliance.'

— **David Abram**, author of *Becoming Animal*

'Visceral and highly imaginative.'

— **Rosie Boycott**, the *Independent*

# Also by Martin Shaw

*Courting the Wild Twin* (Chelsea Green Publishing, 2020)

*Cinderbiter* with Tony Hoagland (Graywolf Press, 2020)

*Wolferland* (Cista Mystica Press 2020)

*All Those Barbarians* (Cista Mystica Press 2020)

*The Night Wages* (Cista Mystica Press, 2019)

*Wolf Milk* (Cista Mystica Press, 2019)

*Courting the Dawn: Poems of Lorca* with Stephan Harding
(Cista Mystica Press, 2019)

*The Five Fathoms* (Hedgespoken Press, 2018)

Mythteller Trilogy (Cista Mystica Press):

*Scatterlings: Getting Claimed in the Age of Amnesia* (2016)

*Snowy Tower: Parzival and the
Wet Black Branch of Language* (2014)

*A Branch from the Lightning Tree:
Ecstatic Myth and the Grace in Wildness* (2011)

# SMOKE HOLE

## LOOKING TO THE WILD IN THE TIME OF THE SPYGLASS

# MARTIN SHAW

Chelsea Green Publishing
White River Junction, Vermont
London, UK

Project Manager: Alexander Bullett
Developmental Editor: Muna Reyal
Copy Editor: Eliani Torres
Proofreader: Nancy A. Crompton
Designer: Melissa Jacobson

Printed in the United Kingdom.
First printing April 2021.
10 9 8 7 6 5 4 3 2 1        21 22 23 24 25

ISBN 978-1-64502-095-0 (hardcover) | ISBN 978-1-64502-096-7 (ebook)

Library of Congress Cataloging-in-Publication Data is available upon request.

Chelsea Green Publishing
85 North Main Street, Suite 120
White River Junction, Vermont USA

Somerset House
London, UK

www.chelseagreen.com

MIX
Paper from
responsible sources
FSC® C020471

For Dulcie
*Love, Dad*

# CONTENTS

# SOMETHING TO HANG YOUR HEART ON

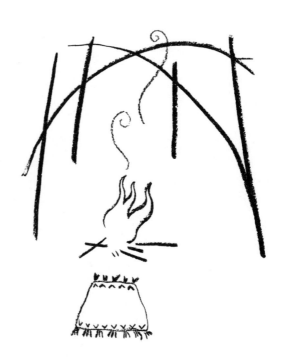

*Once upon a time, there was a kingdom under the grip of a spyglass.*

If you had the spyglass, you could see anything in the world. If you had the spyglass, there was nothing from which you couldn't glean information. It had mesmeric power over the people. It had been created by a king who gave it to his daughter, to be used for the strangest of courtships. If you wished to marry her, you had to achieve only one thing.

You had to disappear.

You had to become a magician of the invisible.

If you could achieve that and defy their magic, she would offer you her hand. If you didn't, you were executed. No one had ever succeeded, and many had tried. It was as if the spyglass secretly longed to be defeated.

But it seemed there was nowhere, absolutely nowhere, the spyglass couldn't peer into. For the longest time, it dragged its hypnotized citizens with it.

But there was a chink in the design. A blind spot.

There was one place that the spyglass couldn't find you.

It was directly under the feet of the daughter.

*Smoke Hole* is a small attempt to meet one infection with another: *beauty.*

What kind of beauty, do you (maybe wearily) ask? The kind we see on Instagram?

Not exactly.

3

I am a teacher of old stories and a guide into deep places. In this life, it would appear I am to be wedded to the *thinking of the wild*. The wild as a regal stretch of Siberian larch, the dark fuse of a Lorca poem, the high clear cry of the hawk. I swoon when I feel it. Then I sober up, pay my libations and study it. My study is a kind of praying. A courting, certainly. It's not bragging; frankly, it's pretty much the only thing I can do. So it's beauty with a salty, old-world panache I really care for.

Beauty kicks-starts our attention. The real sublime. To behold it is almost scary because we suddenly have a longing to stand for something. Beauty not as generic but specific, troubling in what it may call forth in us.

I hope this book infects everyone who reads it. I hope there are soon tangible signs of its impact: you breathe deeper, feel steadier, become acquainted with rapture, held strong in grief. I hope this book is a conduit between the timeless and the timebound, prayer mat and smoke hole.

## Between Prayer Mat and Smoke Hole

Let's start by kneeling down.

Because the thing I'd love to talk about is beneath us. That ground the spyglass can't quite access. It's a little worn, possibly with hurt feelings, but it's there.

It's a prayer mat. We're all praying to something.

I know there's a lot to hold our attention right now – everywhere I glance, there's a screen pummeling us with statistics – but I'm going to ask us to lower our gaze for a moment, you and I.

Examine the weave of the mat; scrunch up your nose and rub up to the dizzy, strange scent of its perfume. There is no one-size-fits-all mat. There are countless millions of prayer mats, and every last one is different. They're just enough room for you to kneel on, and that's about it.

It may not look like much, not with all these other distractions, but we make things holy by the kind of attention we give them. So let's really look at the weave. It's moving. There's a Norwegian tugboat pulling into Alexandria at midnight, there are pale stars over a Provençal castle, there's a desert woman weaving an emu feather into her hair. If we keep paying attention to this little stretch of rug, strange things happen.

We start to witness a secret history of the earth.

Not the only history, but one tributary of a bigger river that eventually leads us to the vast ocean of Time and Consequence.

We behold this with our old mind, not our new mind.

Sometimes I call this Bone Memory. Not skin or flesh, but bone knowing. It's what makes storytellers.

This prayer mat is the stuff of our life. The idiosyncratic, usually shadowed, often neglected root system dwelling patiently underneath us. Not just things we've lived through, but even further back, things our people lived through. Events that, if they were extraordinary enough, got woven into stories, and by a conscious act of memory decided to be remembered.

Let's keep looking.

Behind even your people are swooping cranes, misty Welsh hills, lush Ecuadorian valleys, and miles and miles of flowers. These are your ancestors too.

I say it again: we make things holy by the kind of attention we give them.

In a time when we are begging for a new story, it may be the stories we need are supporting us right now, if only we would lower our gaze.

Many of us don't know it, or more likely have been seduced into forgetting. When you forget what you kneel upon, you are far more easily influenced by energies that may not wish you well.

Well, enough of that.

It's time to kick the robbers out of the house.

I want my imagination back.

And, now we're kneeling, I ask you to do something else.

Look up.

Towards the smoke hole.

The smoke hole reveals to us the timeless, the prayer mat the timebound.

The stories we remember, sink our teeth into – that we never discard, disown, grow too old for – are ones that live in the tension of both timeless and timebound.

The stories that got us and our people here in the shape we are. Those are the timebound. But it's the smoke hole that brings in the timeless, the essential, the vital, and I'm petitioning that we could live between both.

These are edgy times.

As we all know, an invisible pandemic has altered all our lives. Just before we first closed the doors, I sent out a short letter, asking we consider our situation solitude, not lockdown, that there may be some useful magic at hand if we did the work.

There was quite the response.

Thousands of people read the letter, sent me messages, drawings, photos and the obligatory whittled stick (why these keep coming, I do not know).

I include that letter now before we journey further.

## Keeping the Smoke Hole Open

In Siberian myth, when you want to hurt someone, you crawl into their tent and close the smoke hole.

That way, God can't see them.

Close the smoke hole and you break connection to the divine world: mountains, rivers, trees.

Close the smoke hole and we become mad.

Close the smoke hole and we are possessed by ourselves and only ourselves.

Close the smoke hole and you have only your neurosis for company.

Well, enough of that. Really, c'mon. We're grown-ups. Let's take a breath.

We may have to seek some solitude, but let's not isolate from the marvellous.

High alert is the nature of the moment, and rightly so, but I do not intend to lose the reality that, as a culture, we are entering deeply mythic ground.

I am forgetting business as usual. No great story begins like that.

What needs to change? Deepen? What kindness in me have I so abandoned that I could seek relationship with again?

It is useful to inspect my ruin.

7

Could I strike up an old relationship with my soul again?

You don't need me to tell you how to keep the smoke hole open. You have a myriad of ways.

We are awash with the power of words – *virus, isolate, pandemic* – and they point toward very real things. To some degree, we need the organizational harassment of them.

But do they grow corn on your tongue when you speak them?

Where is the beauty-making in all of this?

That is part – part – of the correct response. The absolute heft of grief may well be the weave to such a prayer mat.

Before we burn the whole world down in the wider rage of climate emergency, of which this current moment is just a hint, could we collectively seek vigil in this moment?

Cry for a vision?

It's what we've always done.

We need to do it now.

So, I sent a voice, went to ground, tried to honour what I'd written.

And after a long time of listening, I started to write, and what I wrote you have in your hand. It's what flowered from that original letter.

I should let you know I'm scrawling this in a notebook by a spluttering fire in an ancient Dartmoor forest. I think it's about to piss down. As I am writing, a group of us guides are base-camping seven women and men fasting in the woods. I will almost certainly move between addressing rites of passage and myth, back and forth. A story can be a ritual in words; sometimes a ritual is a story in action. Up here we have a good pile of timber, the coffee is splendid and I can hear a screech owl some way back in the brush. A little further down the hill, the owls are tawny. This is a byre of deepest contentment for me. It's dusk and the temperature is dropping. I'm just where I'm meant to be.

Now, the stories in *Smoke Hole* are exactly the kind of stories we would tell to prepare the vigilers. And I think we are all on some strange kind of vigil right now. In this book particularly, I am working out of a tradition that belongs to what you could call a commons of the imagination: the fairy and folk tale. These are old stories from Europe and the Caucasus Mountains, doubtless with hundreds of variant tellings. A commons is a place where all are welcome. Come on in, the door's open.

In the last hundred years, fairy tales have served hard time in many therapists' offices. My work is an attempt to bust them out. Too much crowbarring of symbolic theories creates a breathless, even rather lifeless experience. Not always, but sometimes. I hope I haven't done that here. My aim is to react to felt experiences within the story, but leave enough space for you to orientate as well. We've been doing something like this since we first gathered and told stories at all. Wending our way in. Many of my students will study the cultural life and history that infuse such tales, become scholars of the folk knowledge that can reveal itself through all kinds of discreet details. These stories often have a zip code if you look long enough. The vigorously stripped-back quality of a fairy tale gathers energy around its images; you can picture them clearly because of the light descriptive touch. It's not always fashionable to say so, but it's when an image becomes a metaphor that we tend to get really gripped.

9

Whilst fairy tales and the wider myths are far more than metaphors, if we don't really grasp metaphor at all, then our current way of life seems all the more unsettling, diminishing, existential.

A good metaphor is something you can hang your heart on.

It can be the difference between life and death, I'm perfectly serious. In working with young people especially, I've seen this more than once. Things rarely feel true or correct to me until I witness the metaphor in them. I can't trust them. Statistics may have their function, but arriving on an hourly basis into our already depleted brain, they make us crazy.

It was during this cocooning period that the relentless power of social media became more apparent than ever – if we're not terribly careful, it gobbles us up. It has the potential to change our tastes, make us anxious, needy, distracted, not present and, worst of all, have little sense of truth or an integrity of spirit. With the advent of deepfakes and relentless conspiracy theories, we can end up with no sense of what to believe.

*When did a tool become a God?*

It's stories, hewn between prayer mat and smoke hole, that used to get us made. Get us useful, productive, curious, proud when we needed, humble when we needed. We knew we were in one. To feel outside a story would have been a tribal punishment, sometimes even a death sentence.

Stories apprehend our deepest feelings and give them expression, even artistry, before they have to become an external crisis. Intricate old-world rituals performed the same task. They regulated the beneath. They made both performative and magnificent the workings of our psyche.

To keep at it: if affairs of the soul are not recognized as such, they inevitably grow to become crisis and circumstance. A desire to lie still and brood could become a teenage suicide when the youth has not been offered the kind of literacy required to approach the dark storm whirling their heart. This is not a trite observation. I've earnt the statement. Sadly, in my rites of passage work, I have seen the agonies of such societal flatness again and again, and what it does to young people, what it does to their character, their sense of vocation. If all I were exposed to is what currently manifests as leadership, I'm not sure I'd want to make it to adulthood either. As the debates about transgender, climate emergency, BLM are mercifully given more attention than ever before, I still feel that something is missing in the dialogue, something essential: the old stories.

I want to change the pitch, alter the register, offer a different kind of perspective on the times we're in. Most of that gear shift won't come from yet more conceptual high jinks but from very ancient stories and philosophies. Three stories, in fact, stories you can slip in your pocket. And if you feel bereft of that prayer mat, these three are just enough to start you making a weave. Three strands will do it. May you set out on the most magnificent journey.

More than anything, I wish the book to be an ally rather than a persuader, a courtship not a seduction, a place to gather yourself. It is not good to be walking through these times without a story or three at your side.

I've always written for those at a crossroads, and I now find we're all at one.

No more business as usual.

11

It's a time of great paradox: we want to live forever but seem intent on executing the earth. We are technicians of unimaginable advances but are growingly less literate to interpret a way the earth always spoke to us: through myth. I'm wondering if it's time for us to dig up a little chutzpah and send a voice.

*The mess out there is because of a mess in here.*
*Inner and outer talk to each other.*
*That's the truth of things.*
*Let's get to work.*

The reality is that many of us are lonely, disorientated, sometimes afraid. There was no ceremonial announcement for the initiation we were falling into, but I want to offer us three navigational tools for moving forward. *Growing Your Hands Back* – we've been encouraged to touch nothing this last period of time. How do we move back out into the world in a new way? *Breaking Enchantments* – many of us have spent far too long in our own head, stewing in fantasy not imagination. This has to stop. And finally, *Kicking the Robbers Out of the House* – apprehending social media and the internet not as an influencer or saviour but as a tool. Three roads, three strands, three stories.

Keep an eye on where you put the book down – it may have moved when you come back.

## Growing Your Hands Back

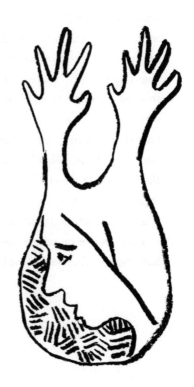

# THE HANDLESS
# MAIDEN

*T*HERE ONCE WAS A MILLER,
his wife and their daughter. There'd been a time
when life had been grand, wealth had flowed like
milk and the wheel of the mill had merrily creaked.
But all that was long ago. On the day our story
begins, the miller was a mile from home, out in
the dark wood. It was dusk, and he was gathering
kindling for the fire. In his scratching for survival,
he didn't notice he'd caught someone's attention.
From behind a tree appeared a man, a very small
man, pale skin, the brim of a hat covering much of
his face. The watcher spoke:

*'Miller, miller, miller. It pains me to see you in this
situation. Truly it does. I remember what good you've done
in the village, the parties you've held, the drinks you've
poured, the poor you've aided. And to see you here today,
scavenging in the grasses for twigs. It's degrading, especially
for a man of such status. I can't bear it, and I can't
imagine how you must feel about it.'*

The miller glanced up for a second and let the cooing land on him. He blinked rapidly in the disappearing light, and the small man continued:

'As a fellow of the wood, I have magic in me. Powerful magic. I'll tell you what, dear miller. As your biggest supporter, let me endorse you. I am going to reverse your bad fortune. From this moment on, anything you desire you can have. Just think it and it's there. The good times are coming back. You and your family will be rich again.'

He now had the miller's full attention, and he piped up:

*'I love this idea. Gods I do. But what would you want in return? You must want something.'*

At this, the fellow of the wood looked thoughtful, as if such a thing hadn't occurred to him.

'Well, for the sheer etiquette of the spell, I suppose I should take some trinket. It is endless wealth I'm giving you, after all. I tell you what: in exchange for all those riches, I will take everything that is behind your hovel at this moment.'

The miller thought for a second: all that was there was an apple tree. Nothing of any significance. I mean, this was the deal of his life.

'Absolutely. I agree. Whatever is behind the home at this moment, you may have.'

At this, a shriek came from the pale man, which he quickly muffled.

'Oh, good for you, *good for you.* I'm delighted to have helped. My spell will be immediate, from this moment, wealth is running back towards you. Scampering, singing, wending its way towards you. I will come next Thursday, to give you a few days to think about the deal, and exactly whom you may have struck it with.'

And with that, he slipped back into the trees, an odd perfume remaining.

It was now almost entirely dark.

Even as he walked back to his home, in the gloom he could see his wife coming towards him, walking fast over the fields, her rough, itchy skirt replaced by an elegant dress, pearls at her neck.

'Husband! Husband! It's a miracle. The kitchen is filled with hocks of ham, strings of onions and garlic, lamb, freshly baked bread, cream cakes and good wine in the cellar. There are paintings hanging on the walls, stacked wood by the fire, a fine new jacket and waistcoat for you all laid out on the bed. How could this happen?'

'Ah, details, details. Now, where is our daughter, so she may share in our good fortune?'

'Why, husband, how could you even ask that question?

'She's where she always is.'

*Behind the house*
*Under the apple tree*
*Sweeping back and forth*

It was then, and only then, did the miller realize the deal he'd struck, and quite whom he'd struck it with.

# The Deal

Have you ever made a seriously bad decision? As is usually the way with fairy tales, we are almost immediately brought to the root of the problem: hard times. A wheel that no longer turns, a generous man reduced to scavenging. When we are depleted, ravenous, jaded, we find we may barely raise our head to see what stands more than a few feet away. We may be only half listening to the deals that we strike.

Every image in a story is an opportunity to bring the scene closer to your lived experience. The storyteller is reminding us of moments when sheer grind brought about lack of discernment, desperation engendered rashness. It is likely that had the miller been in a healthier state, he would have paid keener attention to the details of the arrangement.

But he's shut off and distracted, barely present for most of the conversation. Some believe that the daughter is code for our own soul: that we strike deals that effectively disable the deepest part of ourselves. We gain much in worldly goods, but a dark assassination occurs in our hidden garden. We wince at the image, because we've all lived through some dimension of it.

And she's just a young girl, barely a woman. In fact, likely the age you may have been in an oral culture when you first heard a story like this. Let's linger on that detail for a moment.

In oral cultures, stories like this used to be combed over most intently at adolescence. They were seen as a kind of cloak the youth could shelter under as they wrestled the complexities of puberty, that they had a creel of story to add some form and insight to a very disorientating experience. I'm not claiming that they were some kind of Jungian map, but that in a more free-ranging style they could be quietly chewed on. The youth got smoked in the tale – immersed, troubled, deepened.

And it's no coincidence that I am telling us – you and me – such a story now. Because I have to ask the question:

*How old are we?*

As a culture, as individuals? Not in years but wisdom. This question makes me whistle through my teeth, shift uneasily on my chair. Because I think I know. Deep down I know.

Many of us never quite got over the hump of adolescence. Culturally, that's where we are.

Just the age we should be hearing a story like this, having it work us over. I'm waving at you from my skateboard at almost fifty. Everyone claps for Peter Pan, the boy who never grew up. It's a little pitiful. No matter how much kombucha we guzzle, companies we own, divorces we are assailed by, some part of us remains adolescent. No matter how oiled our hipster beard, how scrambling our 'woke' credentials, much of what we consume feels a little thin. Maybe not catching the dignity of our years.

We could be far less charming than we think we are.

It wasn't always like this. There are parts of the world where becoming an adult was once seen as a complex and invested process. There are dozens of other books (I wrote a few of them) about the values and perils of tribal initiations, so I won't belabour the specifics here. What was vital, however, is how you perceived the world afterwards, and your place within it. You were fundamentally changed, and something self-serving had been willingly laid down. You had banged into an energy far larger than your own ambitions. Majestic, even mystical. The world outside the village. Of deserts, tundra, visions and spirits. The memo was usually that you were to make a joyful labour of your few years here. To be of service to this fleeting awareness. To build a shining house of substance around this glittering seed of longing. To serve. And magically, in that very reduction of *me, me, me,* you became far more yourself. One way or another, you consumed a little humility.

The creation of an adult was a precarious and delicate task, prone to many missteps with a high likelihood of failure. Initiations were attempts not to literalize but exteriorize the kind of wily crisis that life will no doubt hurl at us. It equipped us with an understanding of suffering, vision, doggedness and sacrifice. I am quite aware that doesn't sound sexy. Initiations showed us how to function within discomfort, to stay nimble in the face of paradox. It was a large part of how we got made.

I think this distinction between literalizing and exteriorizing is something to do with intention. Exteriorizing is a conscious enactment of an interior state, in the hope that by demonstration it becomes embodied, less random or chaotic. This is what ritual can serve. By 'interior state', in this case, I mean the psyche's desire to get us shifted from childhood. The soul gets sick of us acting like kids all day long.

Literalizing is what shows up when that *doesn't* happen, and that becomes a possession revealed less by ceremony and far more so by crisis. This is much more common these days. So betrayal, divorce, sickness, depression become the replacements, the wobbly and distracted attempts at learning. That's not to say these things didn't show up in an Indigenous culture, just that there was often a sophisticated ear for working into them. Initiations that made everything less personal. We all like to fetishize our individual struggle sometimes.

In wilderness rites of passage, I've seen this again and again. When the psyche's murmurs are not attended to, it will work out a big, bad public iteration to get our attention. This is less superstition, more just how life works. What we don't sift to consciousness rolls in as drama. To some, this is old news, but also news we constantly and determinedly forget.

A key ingredient to a successful rite of passage is the awakening of *awe*.

Awe humbles. And the idea is to make a home for that awe. An awe that floods our nervous system with largesse, wild geese rippling the depths of our nature. Something that's hard to get over.

Returning to the story, in 'The Handless Maiden', I think the miller has lost his awe, even his animal sense that he's in danger. He's numb, isn't he? And when you're numb, it is far more likely you will experience literalization over exteriorization. He's not conscious, and so gives away without thought the most precious thing.

In the Arthurian epic *Parzival*, the young knight Parzival receives a very strange piece of advice from an older warrior:

*Never lose your sense of shame.*

To a modern ear, this is ghastly. Horrible. We spend thousands of dollars trying to lose our sense of shame. But the old warrior is pushing us towards an initiated awareness of things, a very sensitized awareness. That there are things in this world that really qualify as holy. An oak grove, the twinkle in a baby's eye as it grabs your finger, a bobcat suddenly turning in a Northern California dusk. Fierce awareness of the sacred is what the warrior is getting at. Appropriate humility. A mode of behaviour. Decency. Knowledge of our own occasional lack.

Some readers will still rail at the word *shame* for the example, but if I remove it, I extract the stinger from the thought and it has less energy. That there are ways to behave in this world, and that we are still sensitized enough to know when we have come up short. When we have given free rein to malice, envy or just sheer narcissism.

Whether we linger on *shame* or *awe,* I am suggesting what we have at the beginning of our story is someone simply not present. There is little awareness of the clear and present danger ahead. He is not paying attention. The metaphorical potential is embarrassingly apparent here: miller as government, miller as parent, miller as *you.* As I always say when approaching story, don't let yourself off the hook. I have sold myself short on countless occasions: betrayed principles, friends, myself – simply because I wasn't paying attention.

You know how dogs sniff things? The miller should have sniffed out that situation. Of course, when the ambrosia of flattery worms its way in, it can be hard to turn our head away. A lack of shame means ambition trumps decency; we self-serve and skip off before cost can be counted. A lack of shame lifts the ideas of others into our own mouths and we claim origination. A lack of shame creates a counterfeit life. But what happens when life itself seems to be giving us counterfeit directives? We'll come back to that in the next section of the book.

*T*HE DAUGHTER TOOK THE NEWS soberly, almost as if she expected it. Even as the affluence came raining down, she seemed to withdraw into herself. Amongst all the frivolity, she was focused on something no one else could quite see. On the day the man of the wood arrived to collect, she bathed, put on a white dress, and drew a chalk circle around her. She stood calmly at the circle's centre, and gazed levelly at him.

It was the strangest thing. No matter how he tried, he could not enter the circle. He dodged this way and even leapt frantically in the air, but he simply could not enter her circle. After twenty minutes he was spent.

'Miller,' he wheezed, 'this was not the arrangement. Not the deal at all. She's too clean, too pristine, too contained. I can't bend her. I will return in one week's time and expect her muddied by this world: grimy, bedraggled, broken even. I'll have no problem whisking her off then.'

Feeling the unmentioned threat of consequence, the miller forbade his daughter to bathe, removed the chalk, encouraged her to rub mud on her skin, weave twigs and ivy in her hair, to stink. He and his wife took no pleasure in this, but were simply terrified. This is called being in way over your head.

The day came and shuffling down from the treeline came the pale man with the hat covering half his face. He initially looked pleased at the state of the girl, but as he walked towards her, she started to cry, to really weep. Not tears of fear, but of grief. She wept as we weep once or twice in our life. Tears that carry amniotic fluid and sea salt and the dreams of the sirens in them. Tears that push all before them, that hurl truth, sorrow and defiance into this world, all at once. As she wept, she wiped the tears over her bruised and muddied body. As the tears made tracks, her skin started to gleam. Clean and bright again.

Oh, and so moon bright it was, it was as if that chalk circle had returned. For the second time, the creature could not get his hands on the girl.

'Miller,' he snarled, 'this was not our arrangement. I wanted the smear of the world on her, depressed and filthy. She's not depressed, she's grieving. It's the hands. It's her hands that reach out towards joy and fulfilment, that wiped her body clean with those tears. Get rid of them. Take a silver axe and cut her hands off. You must do it. And if you don't, not only will the wealth disappear, I will bring a killing blight to the village, and your name will be ruined. This is your very last chance.'

As he angrily walked away, the daughter turned
to the miller and said this:
*You were my gatekeeper,*
*And you let in the wolf.*
'Do it.'

The silver axe was gathered, and with all his
might, the miller brought the axe down on his
daughter's wrists.

A week later the being loped from the woods
a third time. He saw the Handless Maiden's
stumps and rejoiced. He saw the destroyed
miller, the emaciated mother, and he rejoiced.
He peered and sniffed and spat on the ground.
And for a second time she started to weep, and
it was as if those tears had an agency of their
own, they moved around the girl's body without
even the use of hands; like lively rivers, surging
creeks, sparkling streams. There were salmon in
those tears, deep-sea secrets, the defiance of the
shipwrecked. The tears washed her clean again,
top to bottom, resplendent.

She stuck her chin up. *Fuck you.*

Well, even fellows from the woods seem to
know you have to give up on the third attempt. It's
just a thing.

Muttering curses we can't quite decipher, he
turned and shuffled across the darkening. An odd
detail: the strangest thing was that the wealth
continued, the deal didn't break. And no curse on
the house. Except maybe the worst.

One night, whilst her parents feasted, the
Handless Maiden slipped away into the dark forest.

*You were my gatekeeper,*
*And you let in the wolf.*

When an old story says she wandered for four
days in the forest, that could be four months
or years. And wander she did. In circles mostly.
There were no fellow travellers, no cheery
firesides, no tales of encouragement and fortitude.
The only trail she encountered was the one she
made by walking it. When she slept, her dreams
were sour and disorientating; when she woke, she
rarely knew where she was. All streams were sluggish, water brackish, and it's hard to hunt when
you have no hands. Occasionally a bird would leave
a little something to chew on. She'd gratefully
gobble it down, belly tight and diminished, stuck
to spine like a tight little drum. The forest had at
her, from every direction. After a time you'd be
hard-pressed to tell if she was a woman, a spirit
of the forest, a wolf, so altered was she. The
trunks of the trees were like prison bars, and she
longed for a wide, open view. But, like her father
the miller, she had to keep her eyes close to the
ground, looking for kindling. It was a diminished
world she peered out at.

For a long time, it stayed like this, exactly like this.

## Old Mind and Deep Woods

The chalk circle, the white dress, the roaming tears – there is no indication that the girl was versed in protective magic, but in a time of ghastly vulnerability, this ceremonial savvy sometimes assembles. Her old mind steps forward. I don't encourage trauma as a spiritual technique, but we all catch the undertow of what's being shown. The maiden displays boundaries, moves to grief not depression, and when the time comes makes the terrible sacrifice. All the way through, she negotiates what she can and, even though grievously injured, is not whisked away by the being from the woods.

Many initiations begin with an act of severance, and this is one of the most extreme examples. Because of an act of inattention by a parent, this savage energy has ripped through the family. Things will not be OK anymore. Whatever life she had dreamt for herself, this was not it.

Another association is of the daughter as the earth itself. That through catastrophic distraction and lunatic ambition, we have wounded it beyond measure. That we as a culture have struck a bargain with an energy that absolutely does not wish us well. It is not to be discounted that this is a grievous blow to the feminine. In myth, men are sometimes wounded in the thigh area; here, with this woman, it's her hands. We can all make connotations of the significance. Her hands that paint, break bread, bring pleasure, strike a villain, pull a vegetable from dark earth, reach out towards the world.

Working with at-risk teenagers, I've met dozens of Handless Boys and Handless Girls, who for one reason or another had been catapulted from their homes into street gangs and crime. These are not kids running wild; these are kids running feral. Big difference. Any attempts at formalizing their traumas into initiations – remember the earlier notion of exteriorizing – are created by their peer group, not experienced elders. There's more than a wobble when all you have to go on is your own age group.

Even so, some of these young people are the bravest, wiliest, most gallant and flat-out inventive people I've ever met. They have looked suffering in the eye and absorbed it, they have shared a bed with discomfort. They've been where we don't want to go. They are veterans, young. It happens. And not all make it, not by a long shot. Whatever disables the psyche is a hand cutting. Whatever derails our capacity to reach out and touch life is a hand cutting. It can be very insidious, doesn't have to come with violence or deprivation, but can lurk in the most privileged of situations.

Everyone who reads a story like this experiences it a different way. For some it's intensely personal; for others, a symbolic field played out on the vastest governmental level possible. Try and track where you go with it.

I would argue that the being from the forest is a spirit that the West made a deal with thousands of years ago, and we have been living in its consequence ever since.

We are in the presence of rapid, almost lunatic technological advancement, and growing absence of what could constitute soul – personal and cultural. The Romantics rallied on this point constantly, but it's clearly a hardy perennial. Maybe only through disaster could something be done. Without that, it's simply too worthy to halt our love affair with *stuff*. It takes the Goddess of Limits to arrive to really sober us up.

I think we've had a rumour of her arrival during the cocooning of lockdown. Likely not enough to quench our desire for things to 'get back to normal', but a rumour, maybe a tremor. And for those who have lost loved ones, far more than that.

I hinted earlier at what I called 'counterfeit directives'. Now would be a good time for me to pipe up with a major one.

*You can be anything you want to be.*

No, you can't.

Not from your old mind's knowing. You weren't born to be anything you want; you were born to be something quite specific. There is a spiritual directive to your life that was assigned somewhere else before you were even born. There's a vocation to your years, even if they appear unremarkable to the rest of us. This is not a status-driven affair. This is a soul coaxed into listening. To be 'anything you want' is part of the chloroform of the anthropocentric, the usual empirical ambition dished out from toddlerhood to many of us. That doesn't mean you don't stretch and change as you age, but that you built on an essential, not societal, sense of vocation. The Greeks used to think of this as your daemon. Part of a wilderness vigil is to attend deeply to that thought, to clear through the tyranny of choice until you really get a sense of how to proceed. From a terrible way of looking at it, hand cutting has just placed a major limit on her life's possibilities. So the hysteria of exponential growth has been replaced by the necessity of depth.

When you leave a comforting hearth fire to enter the dark forest, you usually have to be shocked into doing so. Do you remember Odysseus encountering his men among the lotus eaters? There's a whole island of people effectively enspelled by the sedative rapture the fruit provides – a kind of opiate. It often takes *event* to leave all that surety. As modern readers, we know the story is giving us clues about our life now – from climate emergency to a bewildering invisible disease. The house the West has magicked up is looking shakier than ever. It seems wiser to push into the midnight grasses and the forest rather than abide in recumbent staleness. By something being removed, even so terribly, something may now enter.

The time in the forest is exacting, specific, often nightmarish. There's no time limit set, no stopwatch, no app counting down the seconds and cheering you on. You are on intermittent fasting, whether you like it or not. The sheer grind of it may seem eternal. I think I entered it once or twice in childhood, but the full immersion was waiting in midlife. The great testing. These are ordeals that fundamentally rewire you. Any lover of stories has come across some image of such a forest challenge or being subsumed in the belly of the whale or lost on the ice floe over and over. We may be titillated by the images, but on the day our number is called, we will hold on to the stories as a sailor grips a plank when the foaming waters swirl.

When lockdown began, I was frequently asked to provide stories and perspectives to chivvy people along, to give them a sense of hope. My response was that it was too soon. The evangelical is not the appropriate tone when lost in the forest. That even as we plummet, we are planning our exit strategy. It's a very natural thing to do, but lostness has its purpose. I needed to listen. A lot of listening, wailing, quietening, gnashing goes on in the forest. Within a wilderness vigil,

I've seen hundreds of people rather like you or me formally enter a ritualized version of her journey. And I know, to this day, even now, the forest talks back to them. May take some discomfort, but there's often a return message.

We can all list writers who create under duress, artists who swing in and out of madness, many creatives who have cottoned onto the fact that art constructed in our parents' house is often bland, rather untested. I don't encourage disorder as a lifestyle choice, rather a skill set for when the wolf eats our horse and we are far from the village. Little of substance gets forged without pressure. Duress can birth ingenuity.

To recap the tale for a moment: a figure of authority has made a very bad deal due to not paying attention, a deal that will superficially give him much, but actually remove what he most cherishes. The house is collapsing even as they feast, and their daughter cannot bear the hypocrisy a moment longer. Far into the bleak tangles of the forest she has journeyed.

*O*NE *NIGHT SHE WAS SUDDENLY* at the other side of the forest. There'd been no warning, no preamble, but there she was. The trees were behind her, and in the night sky was a vast yellow moon, full as the face of a coin. Underneath the moon was a castle, an orchard and, surrounding both, a moat. She could see the trees were swollen with apples and pears, even from a distance. Oh, she was desirous of such fruit. It made her skip

31

foot to calloused foot, imagining their taste. Even as she had the sensation, she felt cautious to leave the shelter of the trees. So strange – all she'd done was fantasize about leaving, and now she hesitated. But in the end, both hunger and curiosity prevailed and she stalked her way down to the moat.

They say that the waters of the moat parted for her, a Red Sea moment. They say that trees shuffled forward in the dark earth, such was their ambition to feed her. They say she reached up with her bandaged stumps and pulled down a pear. When she'd consumed it, caution moved through her again and she scuttled back to the treeline. Not into its depths but at the edge of both the royal lands and the forest.

She'd been spotted, glimpsed by a gardener who worked by the moon, not the sun. He'd seen the strange unfolding. He wondered at it all, and next day reported it to the king, a young man who loved unusual stories. The king had the habit of many sovereigns, which was to count his fruit every morning, and he'd noticed one was missing. Well, this was the gardener's moment, so he told the story with full aplomb, and the two of them elected to go back to the orchard that very night and see if she returned.

She did, and the king asked her, gently and with full curiosity, quite who or what she was: a woman, a spirit of the forest, a wolf? She thought on it, chewed on it, bent her soul to it and replied:

*'I'm not sure. I've spent so very long in the forest I just don't know anymore.'*

That's the response of a grown woman.

Some say that the king fell in love with the
Handless Maiden despite the wild hair, wolfish
stance, circling crows. I tell you that's nonsense.
The king fell in love with her *because* of the wild
hair, wolfish stance, circling crows. He thought she
was the most fascinating creature he'd ever met.

The king offered her quarters in the castle,
plenty of space to rest and gather herself, and she
accepted. She could see the forest from her bedroom
window and felt sufficiently recovered to enjoy this
next stage in her journey. Journey to quite what, she
had no idea. It won't surprise you that every day, the
lovestruck young king would take a little tea to her
door, maybe some musicians, good food. He adored
her. He started to work on poetry of varying quality,
and one day his heart forced him to make his big
gesture, standing before her and saying:

*In your bright braided tresses*
*There is a flock of songbirds,*
*Your eyes are like keen crystal,*
*Set in a ring.*

*Your cheek is red like the coal of a fire,*
*And your mouth speaks old words,*
*Like the roar of the waterfall.*

*You are whiter than the swan on the pool,*
*More tuneful than the fiddle,*
*You are a ship on a mistless wave.*

*When I saw you,*
*I thought the moon herself had*
*Fallen into a bed of wild flowers*

*And was singing an old song*
*I had waited my whole life*
*To hear.*

She fell ardently into the fur of his words, and a love affair began. The castle was a place of fresh, sparky life and laughter, the king's mother adored the young woman and it wasn't too long before a marriage proposal spilled from the mouth of the king. She accepted.

As a wedding gift, her husband gave the Handless Maiden the one thing she clearly did not have – a pair of hands, painstakingly crafted from silver – meant quite sincerely. She felt his good will, but rarely wore them.

After a time she felt different: expanded, assaulted, blessed. She was pregnant.

She would sit by the fire with her husband, deerhounds at their feet as they speculated on this new life growing inside her. They tried out baby names and giggled into the small hours. So deep the bliss, it was a vile wrench when the king was called to war at the edge of the kingdom. It was his first war, and the eyes of his people were on him to prove himself. He had to lead from the front. He left with heavy heart and the condition that if his wife were to give birth in his absence, the castle

34

was to send their speediest rider to him to relay the news to wherever he may be fighting.

Though she missed her husband, the pregnancy went well and the Handless Maiden gave birth to a cherubic little boy. Happy hands, happy feet, merry little face, ready for mischief. The speediest rider was sent for and he sped out over the drawbridge, seeking the king.

# Orchard

And, of a sudden, she's out of the forest. Every time I have told this story, this scene resembles a woodcut in my imagination. There she stands in the treeline, half-wolf almost, with a full moon, castle, orchard and silvery moat. Absolutely alchemical. In the Persian world, the word for *orchard* is often associated with paradise. Hell to heaven, all of a sudden. The waters part, the trees lean in and a saintly observer beholds the moment. The wonderful gardener who plants by the moon. We have clearly begun some other chapter in the journey; everything smells different, brackish water replaced by sweet fruit, freezing rain to gentle, moonlit breeze. It's a huge change of set. From uncertain terrain to the calm of a maintained orchard.

We recall that it's a young king (in other words, an energy still growing), who's still open to the world beyond the castle gates, still curious. Many older kings in such tales are corrupted by power, but not this lad. He is aswoon for her. Not as a project or a rescue mission but as something he's simply never seen before. Some kind of simmering, unruly mystery stands in front of him. He's spinning in a dark, delicious, wondrous new world. That feels like a good confluence to me, forest energy and young sovereign. Do you remember the detail that he counts his apples? This is a little shorthand to describe one of the jobs of a sovereign: to keep account. I think once he meets his beloved, he's going to forget the counting altogether.

And what does it feel like when you can't remember if you're a woman, a wolf or a spirit of the forest? There's a refreshing poly-perspective to both the questioning and the answering; the energetic remains dynamic, not settled.

*I just don't know anymore.*

To invite a being like that into the castle is not the same as a Lady, or Princess. This woman looks like *anything-could-happen*. She's already missing her hands, has crows' nests in her hair. The royal is inviting ambiguity and mystery into his very home. This is not an act of political expediency or protocol, quite the opposite. Even in the earlier grotesque attempt to tame her by the removal of her hands, she appears to have more life force than anyone else in the tale. As I've written on several occasions, whenever culture is in peril, the answer usually arrives from the margins, and its manifestation is rarely demure. I light a lantern every night and sit patiently in my garden waiting for such an encounter. It's called being a writer. The Handless Maiden doesn't arrive like Boudicca; she's less strident, more liminal, still-in-change. But in a world breathless with tradition, her presence refreshes, pushes the imagination around. Not as trinket or a wheeled-out amusement but as a totem of magic-in-extremis. She's not a ghoul waving her stumps about and calling it art; she's a woman who has dragged herself through hell on earth and is still deepening, still travelling.

If you identify with her entirely and only as a human woman, he as a human king, you are missing the point, and may struggle with this book. That's only the initial layer. These characters are formidable powers that tear furiously in and out of our lives wherever we perch on the spectrum of gender. It's useful to identify with these stories, but that should over time deepen into other psychic realities than the push and pull of gender relating. That's above-ground stuff, and most fairy tales swim in deeper tributaries. I would not have lasted with them were that the summation of their wisdom. So this is a gentle push not to equate with her needing rescuing or him obliging; we should work up a greater sweat than that, give the story more room. There is a young king in everyone, a wild woman too. We should submit to the swirl. There are some very ancient roots to this story that are likely not human at all.

Do you remember I said we should look to meet the pandemic with an infection of beauty? Maybe that beauty looks a little like the Handless Maiden.

Beauty is not just Botticelli cherubs, not just orderly rose gardens and wandering peacocks; sometimes it looks like nothing you've quite seen before. Its function is not to reassure but provoke. Sometimes beauty can be so startling you may not even recognize it as beauty. There is a medieval tradition of the Loathly Lady, a being that wanders lonely forest paths on a nag, often with tusks, paws of a lion, ears of a bear. Loathly

Ladies are erudite, terrifying, maybe even holy – a famous example being Cundrie, defender of the Grail. The stories suggest that, if she wants you, you should agree to marry her.

These phenomenal beings are emissaries of the wild, and usually possess several shapes. They flip in appearance, depending on how you respond to them. One of the points of the encounter is to make an accord with more than the domestic, the expected, the by-rote. That you are wedded to the wild. To be wedded to the wild means some part of you – maybe a large part – guards your solitude like we guard an endangered owl, tells stories as much for the benefit of the lively dead as the moribund living, makes wayward choices many view eccentric, is capable of sustained generosity, has flashed your teeth and counted cost, has dragged meat back to the cave under the moonlight, has stalked all of Russia with only a line of Anna Akhmatova for company. To be wedded to the wild means you have curated a doorway beyond societal expectation or the perpetual, grinding tic of acting nice. That you have recognized discipline as the essential companion of wildness, that sobriety and ecstasy have made a pact. That's how good art gets made.

In the story we have the interesting development that the maiden takes rooms in the castle. Willing to accept the king's offer, and the change in situation. She is not so habituated by the dark forest she feels she must stay there, but remains alert to movement. I love this.

A rite of passage is just that, a *passage* – it's leading somewhere. There is always the chance in our own lives that we become *perpetually* marginal, *perpetually* hermetic, rather than the labour of functioning between the differing ambitions of both forest and village. Most interesting teachers are crossroads people; they have counterweight in their thinking. A kind of subtle tension that life tends to bequeath and they encourage. Simple answers don't always cut it. Any insight I may have tends to come from solitude, but it deepens again when I go through the difficulty of communicating it to a human community. I know many brilliant people who abdicate that responsibility, preferring to remain hidden in the woods. It's usually just those folks we need to hear from.

Ghastly as it sounds, we can get stuck in disorder, stuck in chaos, it can become habitual, even addictive. But the story tells us it's OK to take lodgings in a castle, to fall in love with a king. That we walk muddy prints over the carpet, submit to a luscious bath of milk, maybe sleep for twelve hours on silk sheets. Good for her. Most crucially this gives her time to catch up with herself, to draw breath, to gather herself in an environment that is wishing her on. That's not to say the forest didn't, but not every breath is a rabid scrap for existence, a walloping tussle for survival. We locate some gentleness entering now, after the earlier horrors and terrible testing.

The crafting of the silver hands is a rookie mistake by the king, well-meaning but not really to be pursued. It gets me to thinking about what we get offered to sublimate wounds to our own nature. Are many of the technological trinkets we now surround ourselves with sometimes attempts to screw silver hands over our stumps? Are they chloroforming some earthy intelligence? Are we prepared to trade relationship to psyche for the absorbing, even hypnotic, chatter with smart tech? What is it concealing, our never-ending spewing forth of high-end gadgetry? I hope you detect the tone: it's not a rant I'm invested in, but a questioning. Silver hands have no warmth, no myriad of nerve endings, no real emotional intelligence, even when presented by a king. She's right not to wear them too often.

To accept the silver hands is to prematurely halt the process you're in, the maturation of it, the *initiation* of it. Don't obscure the stumps; keep peering into the wound, even if that's harder for others to witness than a pair of shiny silver hands. It's an artifice, a covering up, a distraction ultimately. And she sees all that, doesn't judge her lover too harshly for it, but neither is she seduced.

Whenever we give ourselves entirely to love, it seems we start a war. That's a big statement. What I'm suggesting is that the entirety of committing to our feelings makes us drop our boundaries and become ripe for invasion. We lose focus on anything but our beloved. We forget to reply to emails, ignore our friends' texts, the zucchinis pile up in the garden and start to rot. From a storied eye, the responsibility of the sovereign and the sensuality of the lover are usually rather at odds with each other. There's a reason Guinevere can't stop glancing at Lancelot, Isolde can't stop meeting Tristan in the orchard at midnight. The sheer weight of being a queen or king is resolutely non-erotic. So in our story, like so many others, the husband is called to a far-off war as a baby grows in the maiden's belly. We are heartened at least by the detail that she is loved by her mother-in-law. For a while, however, the couple have two opposing functions: the king is to take life, the queen to nurture life.

Pregnancy, holding relationships together, babies – the whole thing is a hugely mythic endeavour. I suggest wrapping as many wise stories around such a task as you possibly can; you're going to need them. Despite what people may say, don't be afraid of the heroic on occasion – you will certainly have to draw from that ancient well of sustenance.

So, something is growing in the maiden, and after all that duress, that flat-out horror, something is coming to get born. Where once something was taken away, now something is arriving.

*FTER A TIME, IT JUST SO* happened the rider found himself back in the woods where our story began. And the strangest thing came over him. A fatigue, a walloping exhaustion, a deep, mysterious drowsiness. He leant up against an oak and rested, his horse munching grass. He was barely conscious – almost dreaming – when a small, pale man with a large hat slipped out from behind a tree and spoke:

*'Speedy rider. You will tell the king an abomination has occurred. That the queen has not given birth to either a boy or a girl, but a dog, a terrible hound. That's what you get when you marry a woman of the forest. Tell him this news.'*

The speedy rider woke from his trance, took in the message and rode like the devil to the tent of the king. The king urgently received the rider and listened to the message intently. He grew quiet and looked out over the battlefield, gazing at the piles of dead warriors who would never see their families or home again. He chewed hard on his thinking. Finally he turned:

*'Though this is not the news I expected, still I welcome it. Whatever has come from my wife's womb will be loved by me, whatever its shape. Tell my beloved that I am humbled that she is so delightfully full of surprises, that I will be back the moment I can, and that my heart bangs wild under my breastplate with joy.'*

After some venison and beer, the rider rode back over the heath and into the forest with the message, wondering at the maturity of the king. Ah, but after a time, a weariness came over him, didn't it? A need to rest by the old oak tree, under its lush bough. His horse munching grass, he barely noticed when a small, pale man with a large hat slipped out from behind the very tree he was slumped against:

*'Speedy rider. You will tell the queen mother that he is appalled that such a demonic abomination has occurred, that he will not suffer it to live, nor his witch wife. That he expects the heart and tongue of his wife presented to him on a plate on his return from war. Tell her this news.'*

The speedy rider woke from his trance and rode like the devil to the castle of the queen mother. The queen mother heard the message and grew quiet, looking out of the window a time before she spoke.

'It is clear that the brutality of war has sent my child utterly mad. This is ludicrous and nothing of the sort is going to take place. However, what is clear is my daughter-in-law and my grandson are no longer safe. Please summon them.'

When they were all gathered together, the queen mother told the Handless Maiden a hard thing. That she and her son would have to venture back out into the forest until this horrible episode was cleared up and it was safe for her to return. At this, the maiden wept, shuddered and grew pale at the thought. But her mother-in-law was sage and kind, saying:

*'I know, I know. But I tell you this. The dark forest is never quite the same the second time around. Believe me. It isn't and it won't be. Take courage, gather yourself, and you will surprise yourself. But for now, it is urgent that you leave.'*

Early the next morning, a hat concealing most of her face, the maiden and her child slipped into the treeline and disappeared.

## Fake News

This is a story walking us in several directions. Whoever said time was a straight line? We now find ourself right back at the beginning, in the very woods the terrible deal was struck. A message is caught and manipulated between king and queen, warrior and mother. Fake news flying around the psyche. When we are out of touch with truth, we can stew on such wretched and fictitious messages. Often in a fairy tale when a witch or sorcerer wants to infect you, they get you alone and start whispering such distortions in your ear, designed to paralyze your immediate relationships. The mythologist Marie-Louise von Franz called this 'cold evil' as opposed to 'hot evil'. Hot evil is all giants and swinging clubs, heads on spikes, villages massacred, very visible. Cold evil is something else again. Very interior, very subtle, very whispery, very hidden. This is a good example. It has a hallucinatory, paranoid essence. Gossipy.

This messenger serves the god Hermes (as they all do), but lacks his deity's discernment. An interesting detail about Hermes is that he carries news 'soul-to-soul', so if the soul is not roused, the message is not received. What is so alarming in modernity is that we have the speed of Hermes, but may lack the integrity of the messaging. We could be getting spun by almost anything. Of course, humans have conjured up such distortions for thousands of years, but not with such a platform for mass entrancement. Every election now seems a masterclass in fiscally plumped, Wi-Fi-cranked mirage-speak. We do well to know when the man with the hat is whispering in our ear. You may be working to the point of burn-out and are far distant from your child and partner. That's a moment when messages get all twisted up and a hostile forest springs up between you. Cold evil. We owe Ms Franz for our ability to name it.

What's so admirable is the king's response to the news. He rolls with it. I didn't see that coming. No hissy fit, no 'What will the neighbours think?', just care for his wife and adaption to circumstance. The man's progressive. This is one of the story's great aikido moves: trouble comes at you, and rather than striking back you disable it by moving in an unexpected fashion. It's Tricksterish in its way. You neutralize the poison by your own unpredictability.

Of course, it's harder to negotiate on the return journey of the rider. But thankfully, the queen mother has no intention of playing out such a grotesque request. She catches sulphur's whiff. But what she hefts onto her daughter-in-law's shoulders seems quite terrible – a return to the forest. A return to uncertainty, cold, discomfort, fear. The only bit of sustenance in such a dark decree is that the forest is never the same twice. But for the young woman, again it seems that her story is starting to move backwards. No security, no status, no loving environment for her baby, but the bleak and barbarous forest.

*N*EVER QUITE THE SAME THE *second time.*

Towards the end of the day, the maiden did indeed see something she'd never set eyes on before in the forest: a friendly trail of smoke. Someone was out here too. Someone else was surviving in this environment. She followed the smoke, baby in her arms, till she saw its source. It was coming from the chimney of a rustic cottage.

She could hear rascal laughter, cheery singing, so she peered through the window. She could see women, many women, of all ages. Some were gathered by the fire, some knitting, some cooking, gossiping – the mood seemed wonderful. They spotted her peering in, and the door was swiftly opened. She was emphatically gathered in, with all cooing over the moon-faced babe. From the moment she sat with them and powerfully recounted her story, it was clear she had found a new home, in the exact place that she was most terrified to go to. These stalwart women were called the Wood Sisters, and gathered under their shawls, they had a great understanding of the inner rhythms of the forest. Things grow in a cottage like that, things get better, even cautiously recover.

*And a great wonder happened*

*A joy beyond reckoning*

She started to grow her hands back. Bit by bit. It could have been the first time she defended her child or stood naked in the storm, or wrestled a root from the soil, but she started to heal, right there. Not as a solitary hero fighting a dragon, but right there in the fine company of the Wood Sisters. And it is a powerful thing for a young lad to grow with a cackling flank of jubilant aunties around him. For some years it continued like that, lively and restorative, but I cannot tell you that the maiden did not wonder what had happened to her husband. I cannot tell you she didn't gaze out at dusk, make a bed for her sorrow.

And what of her husband? When he returned, jubilant and expectant to meet his wife and dog-child, he was stricken with terror when presented with the heart and tongue on the plate (those of a doe). When his mother saw that there must have

been subterfuge in the messaging back and forth,
she told her son everything:

*'And now she and your boy are out there in the forest. It
is up to you to find them. I thought they had to go there for
their own protection. But now I wonder if it is indeed you
who needs to go there. I'd always wondered on the imbalance
of forest knowledge between you and your dear wife. It is
your turn for the great wandering, my dear son, and I wish
you wisdom and protection as you go.'*

Having not even removed his mud-caked cloak,
his sword and belt, the king turned from his
mother and rode wearily alone into the forest. He
did not behold the trail of smoke on the first day,
or the second, or the third. He beheld sodden
flanks of branch and leaf, drizzling mists, tracks
that led nowhere. He beheld nightmares, blustering
and endless snowstorms, ravenous black bears and
any number of sorrows hanging on him from the
battlefield. A year turned into two into three and
onwards. After seven years, his hair and beard fell
to his waist, hands nicked and scarred, barely recognizable from the buoyant young sovereign of years
past. There was a weight to him, a seriousness. And
still he searched, way past the time when most of us
would have retired from such a hopeless cause.

*But comes a day comes a day comes a day*
*When he saw the blue smoke*
*A cottage, the sound of laughter and singing*

Male voices, low and jovial, of all ages. He
caught the scent of cherry tobacco and thought he

47

recognized a folk song. He weakly knocked on the door – just a tap – and it swung open. He was glee-fully gathered in by the men, sat by the fire, a bowl of elk stew and crusty buttered bread, a pint of dark beer. Paradise comes in many forms. And he asked:

'Have you heard of a woman and child, coming this way?'

'Oh, we have, we have. We are the Wood Brothers, and they live with the women we adore, the Wood Sisters, just a mile or so away.'

Word was speedily sent to the women's cottage, and by the end of day, the men could hear the women approaching, singing and dancing, all dressed top to toe, abundant in their finery. The men had scrubbed up well and encouraged each other to be bold in the face of the magnificence of the women. At some point, the tones of the women and the men's singing joined into something quite wonder-ful. And the Woman Who Grew Her Own Hands Back was reunited with the Man of the Deep Places.

For a moment, a veil was held between them, by the oldest woman and oldest man, and then it was dropped.

*And for just a second, they saw each other as God sees them.*

Just a second, but that beholding can be long enough to sustain a marriage when the road is long, awfully twisty and occasionally more than a little mad.

If there was any joy left to attain in the king's heart, he just about exploded when he looked down and saw his lad holding onto his belt, smiling up at him. He gathered him up weeping, then gazed in wonder at his wife's beautiful, restored hands. She smiled:

*'I'll tell you about them later.'*

Of course there was then days of feasting, and everyone fell in love with each other, even the long married. It was a long and happy life for our three.

And how do we know this story at all?

The son of the two of them became a storyteller, and wandered the courts and firesides of old Europe telling the story of a woman who grew her own hands back and a father who never gave up. And he told someone, who told someone else, who told someone else, and I find myself telling the story to you here today.

And I ask you:

*What are you going to do with it?*

*Never quite the same twice.*

We go where we are terrified to go and we find companions. A long-denied glow starts to pour into me at this part of the story. The glimpse of the women in the cottage will always walk with me, the rest of my life. This does an end to the exhausted notion that every trial must always be faced alone. We both know there are moments like that, but not always. And not now. She's done the hard yards and has encountered a whole cadre of women who have done the same, that gather her in, that warm her, that adore what she has brought into the world – her baby son.

For most of us, that scene may be enough, but the beauty is deepened again when she starts growing her hands back in such lively company. She is not tackling a Grendel on a wind-bleak mountain, she is not scrambling around in the belly of a giant, she is supported, cherished, even healed. This is momentous – that community need not cancel out individuation, but actually support it. That a group of women can gather in their collective experience of the forest and grow wise, not bitter, robust with agency, not isolated and privy to figures that whisper. And, as we know, there is a group of earthy men just over the way digging into similar ground. These cottages are temples really, inclusive and quite magical.

Again, as contrast, we have the long sojourn of the king. His time in the tangly forest. Even experience of a battlefield isn't the same thing. He's learning more than a thing or two about fidelity. We felt his love of the flighty in his poem to his wife-to-be, but he has iron in his saddlebags now. It could well be this is the equalizer of experience they need for their marriage to actually have a chance.

You may know how it feels when your partner has seen more of the world, tasted more lovers, lived more lives than you? Despite their protestations, that can lead to a seed of imagined inequality growing hard in your belly. You may find yourself listening to false rumours and shivering in the coldness that emanates from them. Please don't linger there. We should check it's not the disorientating paranoia of the Fellow from the Woods.

# GROWING YOUR HANDS BACK

All these images of not cutting hair or wiping tears from your eyes are the material of grief, to do with deepening, to make covenant with loss and the indelible wisdom that sometimes arises from it. That kind of discomfort feels hard to negotiate, but it's material that lasts. Every day that I've been writing this commentary, I go running by a river. Within minutes I am supremely uncomfortable; I'm no athlete. But I do it – as well as for my heart – to make covenant with a little discomfort, to negotiate suffering, mild though it may be. Negotiating a level of suffering is very much part of what initiations have always been about. Life is nothing short of terrible on occasion, and initiations (the orchestrated kind) are an attempt to equip you to stabilize in moments of great stress. Without visible signs that you have undergone that process, you are not understood as a grown man or woman, and you are certainly not to be trusted.

In fairy-tale imagery, this is what the king is demonstrating. That he actually deserves to stand next to the woman who grew her own hands back. And crucially – *underlined* – he is not reliant on her for a relationship to the wild. That marriage, that bond has now occurred within himself. For a life as public as the king's, witnessing him in the privacy of those years alone is meaningful for me.

I think we all sense that the real marriage between the couple is only now occurring, and we are receiving a kind of masterclass in how a marriage could survive, and even flourish. Woven into every scene are the chewy insights of many storytellers with a hand on the tree of good and evil, songbirds flying from their lips.

Don't be afraid to brood on questions like these: How do we help the earth grow its hands back? How do we make a covenant with the wild and the sovereign within ourselves? How do we discern falsity? How do we curate the wisdom that comes from suffering? How do we find wood sisters, wood brothers?

These questions are not self-help in the typical way of understanding the term. They are not self-serving or elementary. They are complex, they're salty. They don't necessarily need a rational response. They are the very stuff of *life*.

And as we come to the end of this story, I send a voice back to the miller and his wife at the very beginning. Those parts of us that have been seduced into actions we deeply regret. I send a voice that peace and reconciliation moved between the parents and their daughter. So many families bear out this story. I send a voice that as cultures, humans, parents, brothers and sisters, whiskery ones, settled ones, unsettled ones, ones that are more crow than girl, more antelope than boy, the whole lot of us grow our own hands back so this beauteous earth can start to do the same.

If you're going to make a prayer, might as well make it a big one.

*Breaking Enchantments*

# The Sacredness of Defeat

*The mess out there is because of a mess in here.*

A troubled soul makes a troubled earth. Well, there's a very old way of working on that. A kind of open-heart surgery only the wilderness can offer.

As mentioned, I'm sitting here by a small fire in early autumn. My low-slung chair is ancient, creaky, reeking of woodsmoke. Above me a yellowed and ragged tarp, held up with several sticks. Lanterns swing. I loathe base camp looking too domestic. I mean I really can't stand it. I'll fire a guide for too much bushcraft efficiency. I can hear the roar of the River Dart to my left, and to my right, scattered further into the woods are several women and men who are fasting for guidance in their life. I didn't quite say clarity, but guidance. It's an ancient way of facing an emergency. Because the guidance they seek is not to do with fast bucks, a better complexion or more followers on Twitter, but a way of being in service to the earth and its habitants. It can be a shattering experience. Breaking enchantments can hurt.

The fire, I have to admit, is giving off more smoke than flame today. I feel a little like that myself. I glance around at my dear team, irascible buddies I've trained to continue the work when I simply can't abide working with the general public anymore. The years have walloped me. There's Tim, sawing up a pile of long fallen branches, Dave is assailing the washing up, and Tina's refilling the water jugs. Soon we will regather around the fire, and to the wee small hours, hold faith for our dear fasters way out there in the Otherworld. We may all be in the same forest, but from the moment we blessed them out, from the way we understand it, they are in spirit time. For a brief period of days, they are unshackled and open to the mysteries.

Joking aside, there's nothing 'general' about the fasters: they've been both screened and counselled to get to this point. What they're doing is high stakes. Four days and nights, culminating in an all-night vigil. Only on the fifth morning do they wend their shaky, eyes-bulging way back to us. In time they will have a story to tell, a hard-wrestled story. Since the far-off days of the Celts, people of this island have sat in remote places and fasted. Listened. All over the earth we find some iteration of this. It's not an encounter I recommend habitually, rather an opening to the irascible, devotedly laboured, tear-whetted maturation of becoming a grown human. And wherever that leads, it's best to start with your arse on the dirt. That way, even for a moment, you may get to witness the thinking of the wild.

Mechanics, taxi drivers, professors, teachers, gamblers, artists, boat makers, even the occasional politician have taken this road with me. From every walk of life, for any number of reasons. And, as they squat by the fire, preparing to head out alone, there are three areas that I am sure to address with them.

## Counterfeit Directives

That you may have swallowed some damaging nonsense here and there. You settle up with everybody and everything that's got you this far. The good stuff you've gained will walk with you the rest of life, but the persuasions and mandates that were toxic, they stay on the hill when you return. This can be extraordinarily effective, but you have to walk some hard yards to receive it, and need a trained guide with you. The way you may get remade in the wild could change everything on your return. Don't go looking for an encounter like this if you have your life (finally) in a calm, sustaining spot. This will likely rattle such peace. Tread carefully when you tread on holy ground. We societally make a fetish of the word *transformation,* sometimes forgetting the question of *into what* on the other side.

## Submission and Defeat

This is not an austerity to fit your schedule. The vigil has a shape you are not to deviate from, a clear and incredibly simple structure. Clean, true, with not a shred of exploitation to it. It's crucial that you trust your guide because you will likely find there's not a whole lot of negotiation when you decide that actually, *hey,* you want to eat a little every day, and move your spot every day, and maybe take a phone for a call or two – at the very least take some photos. You will simply be driven back to your car and invited to come back when you're ready. The reason you can trust the clear boundaries of this encounter is that in the end, the teacher you will meet is non-human. It doesn't look like me. It's the living world. There's no hook in it.

The reek of entitlement that rolls off occasional participants is sometimes profoundly engrained. Frequently their first vigil is simply working on removing the encrusted husk of their unquestioned and now very tedious privilege. The remotest flicker of a boundary, and we see exactly what age they are – adolescent. So it saves us all time to wrestle like Jacob and the Angel with your issues of individuation and being endlessly witnessed ahead of time. Because, actually, what I look for in your eyes when you return is not victory. I'm looking for *defeat*.

That you encountered spiritual energies that knocked you on your back. That surprised you, challenged you and showed you in a hundred different ways the correct size you are in the grand scheme of the earth. That through this defeat you would come to know *awe* again, and never, ever let it go. Reverence leads to participation.

You likely get nowhere near that without defeat. Most of the time when you walk into the forest, you have to quietly lay down the story you've fantasized about having and submit to the experience you *need* to have.

## Waking the Bone Pile

I often tell a story of a young shaman who reanimates a pile of old bones. Suddenly he has a hundred people shaking themselves down in front of him, looking for a home. There's a lot of bones waiting out in the forest for you. Just as you are hoping to lovingly commune with a doe or tearfully call up the sun, there is a rotting pile of ex-lovers and abusive family members leering at you. Down into the muck we go. I frequently see a woman walk out alone into the forest, and ten come back. She's reclaimed her bones. Because there's a great deal of exiled energy in the bone pile. Lots of trouble you'd rather not comb through, but there it is. Go get your juice back. I likely don't need to tell you this is Underworld stuff. Once you get near the smelly bones, you've likely strayed into the part of the forest that Baba Yaga lives in.

Those who glimpse her have said she's a small woman who speaks out of both sides of her mouth. That she has a snakeskin coat and black pitiless holes for eyes. She loves sex and meat and sometimes contorts into a winter storm. Depending on her mood, she is the rain that cools you on a summer's day or the flood that sweeps your house away. There's no telling which way it could go. You likely know that she has a hut on chicken legs that is always turning but also emphatically facing the darkest part of the forest. At night she moves amongst our children and takes their teeth, replacing them with small, dark lumps of iron.

At some point out in the woods, you will likely have to eat some darkness, and Yaga is the one who will just as likely chivvy you along. If you can survive her extreme form of instant discriminations, if you can display enough Underworld sophistication, quicksilver wit, gallows-soaked humour, then she may not just let you live, she may even bless you. Knowledge of Yaga may make your bones not just reanimate, but actually dance. Somewhere out there in the forest, there may well be a bump in the night. That's where all the really good stuff is.

Christ, I feel like I've been doing this since Noah was a boy. Quarter of a century, certainly. It's exhausting, occasionally exhilarating and always humbling, being a wilderness guide. I'm not known for my ability to tie knots, have the most extensive medical kit or ornate whittling skills – I'm known for knowledge of spook.

Over the autumn and winter of last year, I completed a series of 101 ceremonies in this very wood, that culminated in an all-night vigil almost right where I sit. The ceremonies consisted of what I call Calling Songs. Asking for nothing, giving something. The calling was in the form of gifts – ancient stories, poems, libations – and then I would just listen and listen, through the dusk and into the dark time. Such a thing can change you. And it certainly changed me.

It appears you can perk up the mood of a place with a good story. And that fidelity has currency in the wild places. To keep showing up, not taking anything, just being sweet and straightforward with a place, it has an effect. I asked the woods this:

*How do you want me to love you?*

From then on, I just followed that lead. Years before, I'd heard a man, John Lee, talk about the wonder of that question within a human relationship, the good it could do. To no longer crowbar your own sense of how that should look onto another. To actually take a breath and enquire.

I think I told you I felt old. I'm not old. The rocks I have by my boots are old. Tens of thousands of years old, brought up from the freezing shale of a January River Dart. Two rocks I bang together when I need to feel my old mind rebooting, when I'm round that little wet wood fire, more smoke than flame.

And as I keep gazing, I realize something.

The vigilers have become smoke.

For a little while, they may have become shapeless. If they meet a spirit, it may not be in any kind of form they recognize; trees may speak, rooks may whisper. It's rarely a case of strong lines and clear definitions. Hours, dreams, visions, hunger, clarity, all drift in and out of each other. The extreme liminal, you could call it. For me, *spirit time* will do. Suddenly soul is expanded, loping, jubilant. Suddenly soul is not wrapped up with your personality, but enmeshed in rooks, puddles, lamb fur, glaciers, banshees, conch shells. It appears we have to shake the cage a little to get nearer that reality. We don't have soul, soul has us, if we can just register it. So often, I'm that numbed-out miller, gathering his sticks.

So, keep swirling, smoke-people, and do what you must. And when the hour comes, let our base-camp call be clear enough to bring you back down the smoke hole and into the fontanel of the life you are now invited to live.

There's a difference between smoke and fumes, you know. Let's not live on fumes.

Time for another story.

# THE BEWITCHED
# PRINCESS

*T*HERE WAS ONCE A LAD CALLED
Peter. Not a king or a lord, just a man from a hut
that he lived in with his father. Peter was bored. He
didn't have any great plan, just a sense that he needed
to get out into the world, see a few things. He spoke
to his father who understood such a longing, and the
old man gave him his inheritance and watched his
son take the lonely road from their settlement.

It was thirty pieces of silver that Peter now had
in his pocket. He loved to feel the weight of them,
the bulge. More money than he'd ever seen. That
early morning, he walked beyond the world he knew
and out towards whatever his destiny was. He may
have fantasized about meeting a lover, or wrestling
a dragon, but he had no wondering at all for what
actually transpired. He came across a corpse lying
by the side of the road. Maybe a man like him, from
humble beginnings. He stared at the body for a bit,
noticed the crows starting to circle, picked up the

body and staggered with it to the next village. He called out to the villagers that this man deserved a proper burial, but no one seemed to recognize him. Peter had seen this kind of thing before. He took out his purse of silver and offered to pay for the funeral. It was the funniest thing – a miracle – suddenly the entire village remembered the dead man – in fact, remembered him going out to work the fields just that morning. Remembered they loved him, and if Peter just relinquished his purse, they'd see to the funeral. Well Peter did, and it was quite the send-off, with an extended and bounteous wake.

The next day, Peter set off on the road out of town, penniless and a little hungover. After a time, a man walked out from a field in the early-morning mist and started keeping step with him. Peter barely looked to his left, as he knew it was the dead man.

Some hours into hard walking and unable to shake his new companion, Peter arrived at a town. He'd rarely seen a settlement that big, and its appearance was even more unsettling. Everything was black. The tavern sign was black, the ice on the pond was black, even the pale children wore black clothes. A shroud had been flung over the place.

When he asked about it, Peter was told that town was in mourning; that their princess was bewitched by a mountain spirit who lived up behind the houses. That he was her lover and had possessed her. He used her as a rag doll for his desire, which was the death of young men. The way that was achieved was like this: the princess would give three riddles to potential suitors; if they could answer, none of them were executed. Nine of the brightest men in the area were already dead. You went into the princess's castle and never came out. Only the mountain spirit knew the answers to these strange questions that were not really riddles at all, as you'd never be able to guess them.

High stakes indeed, for the hand of the princess.

Even so, Peter resolved to try. With his ghostly companion, he was offered a room at the castle, and then over the following three days the riddles would be delivered. That night, Peter's companion beckoned him over to the window. They saw the princess floating up towards the mountain and her terrible lover. Over the fields she floated, over the swaying pines she floated, over the silvery streams she floated, above it all, high in the dank air.

The dead man produced from somewhere a set of leathery wings that he fitted with straps to Peter and told him to follow. Precariously, Peter set out. High up on the glowering mountain was the entrance to a cave. Peter saw the princess alight and walk into its darkness. A minute or two later, he landed and tentatively followed. It was a gloomy night, just a few stars brocading the way above him. He crept past an altar, but couldn't make out what was displayed on it.

He saw a vigorous-looking man with a long white beard seize the princess and run his hands

all over her. She in turn told him about the arrival
of Peter, and that she needed three new riddles if
they were to kill another young man. The mountain
spirit liked this, and stroked his beard:

*'Think of your father's white horse, all alone in the
stable. Tell the suitor to guess what you are thinking.'*

With that, the spirit's eyes flared up red and
ravenous:

*'The more death you bring me, the more blood you bring
me, the closer we are.'*

What a terrible covenant between lovers.

The next day, Peter went to see the princess.
She was all in black, pale and quiet, as if she had a
secret. She asked him the riddle that is not really a
riddle at all:

*'What am I thinking of?'*

*'You are thinking of your father's white horse, all alone
in the stable.'*

It was as if a funeral bell had struck. She shuddered, and really looked at him for the first time.
She bade him return tomorrow.

That night from his window, he saw her float
up towards the mountain and her terrible lover.
Over the dreams of the people she floated, over the
responsibilities of her role she floated, over even
her identity as a woman she floated. Into the arms
of her lover in the dark of his cave.

Peter's wings were strapped on by his dead
companion, and he flew upwards, stronger this
time, following the princess. He noticed the cave

was a touch brighter, the moon was growing and was making it easier to see. He could just about tell that it was not even really a cave but a large hall, deep in the mountain. This time on the altar he could see there was a fish. The princess ran to her lover and he seized her with his hot hands. She told him what had transpired with Peter, and he quickly shot back with the next riddle:

*'Think of your father's sword. Tell the suitor to guess what you are thinking.'*

Of course, the next day Peter had the answer to the riddle.

The third night he flew up to the mountain spirit's hall, it wasn't just moonlight that had started to illuminate the area but actually sunlight. He could see that on the altar next to the fish was a wheel of fire, turning and sparking bright. Realizing he could be spotted, he hid behind the stone shrine and peered out. Uncomfortably blinking in the rapidly lightening hall, the spirit hissed when he heard the news that Peter had guessed the second riddle. With that, he tugged on his beard, his eyes flashed hot and weird, and he suddenly looked far, far older than he had before:

*'Think of my face. No human can remember something so ancient. Tell the suitor to guess what you are thinking.'*

After that the two lovers were together awhile, and then she left, walking by Peter sheltering behind the altar of the fiery wheel and the fish. When he saw her step into the darkness and float towards the castle, Peter came out from what was left of the shadows and swiftly decapitated the mountain spirit, placing his furious, ancient head in his bag and flying down on those wings the dead man had given him, stronger than ever now.

The next day he was summoned to the princess, and she gave the third and final riddle.

*'What am I thinking of?'*

*'You are thinking of exactly this.'*

And with that, he rolled the head of her terrible lover out of his bag to her feet.

She rolled and she rocked, gnashed and wailed, but some awful energy passed from her body. When she had recovered, she did indeed accept the hand of Peter in marriage. Soon, the shroud was being lifted off the town, the tavern sign was repainted, the ice melted on the pond, the children wore bright colours, the deep silence of the place was replaced by music and chatter, townsfolk were out on the streets again. What a celebration this would be! Just before the wedding night, the dead companion came to Peter:

*'The sweetest thing you can give your wife is this. Prepare her a bath before the two of you make love. When the water touches her, she will become a raven and attempt to fly out the window. Catch the raven and place it back in the bath. When the water touches her, she will become a dove and attempt to fly out the window. Catch the dove and place it back in the bath. After these animal shapes, you will behold your beloved not as a princess anymore, but as a*

*queen. This is my last piece of guidance. From tomorrow, I will have disappeared.'*

The night transpired just as the companion advised, and in the morning, when Peter searched for him, he was gone. From that day forth, the people had a queen with the battle insight of a raven, the gentleness of a dove, and free from all enchantments.

Sometimes a great story doesn't begin with a roar of trumpets or grandness of any kind. This one begins with curiosity. Peter is a little restless, that's about it. He looks at his ageing dad slumbering by the fire and thinks, *Jesus, is this all there is?* Our entrance to the tale is Peter as *all of us* – not a shining knight or divinity masquerading as a human, he's simply the boy next door. The energy levels of the story, the promise of adventure, both are idling rather than in full effect.

As a parent, I've sometimes encouraged my daughter to be bored. You've likely done the same. To just stew a little. Endless stimulation sometimes exhausts rather than deepens imagination. Boredom is not always the enemy. Boredom creates restlessness creates art. That's the way it's been for me, anyway. Peter is not viewing the world through a spyglass; he's actually going to have to go out and find it. He's going to have to cut some ties, take some risks, get lost and start again. For thousands and thousands of years, we've had to do this if we really risk a little educational travel.

Peter at this point is not invoking the high stakes of Olympian myth, rather the more meandering type of homely excursion you find almost everywhere there are humans. Despite his boredom, there's no sign of Handless Maiden–like trauma in his relationship with his father. We see this in two ways: (1) His father's willingness for his son to go journeying. As an old man, he's just lost a great deal of physical help round the settlement. (2) He is able to give Peter thirty pieces of silver. Not thirty rat skulls or thirty kicks in the teeth. So something essential and uncontaminated has passed between father and son. Whatever is best in their relationship is contained within those thirty pieces of silver. Whatever blessing, maturity, wiliness and skillfulness that abide in the father has passed cleanly to Peter. All of that is contained in the gift. So he's not leaving in either anguish or high ambition, rather just a vague sense of instinct. He could be on a gap year or the night bus to New York City – he's a nice kid.

And a nice kid who is immediately thrown into a situation of responsibility he almost certainly did not seek: dealing with a corpse. Have you ever carried a dead body, slung them on your shoulder and stumbled along, maybe for many miles? It's an experience that's never forgotten. Judging Peter as simply a man for a second, it's impressive. He could have skipped over the body and jogged on. It wasn't his responsibility, it wasn't his doing, let someone else handle it.

But, no. Something of his quality is shown. He takes on the burden; he doesn't shirk the event because it doesn't fit his fantasy life of what he expected to happen on the road away from his father. How many of us leave the traditions of our family in attempt to feel freer and are suddenly confronted by something of weight and consequence? Initiation shows young people how to totter beautifully with a sense of vocation by harnessing themselves to something heavier and older than they are – the traditions and rituals of the tribe. On the other hand, we also know youth absolutely overburdened at a cripplingly young age. Within the context of this story, it proves essential, but in modern life, often lacking deeper insights, there's a grotesque side to carrying too much too soon. The family falls apart and there's a thirteen-year-old girl playing mom, her adolescence extinguished in the frantic repair job required to oxygenate the family. Those years – hopefully lofty, bright and filled with possibility – get skipped.

But in the context of this story – and in the wilderness vigil – the weight is appropriate, the sacrifice essential. You could argue that Peter leaves the hut as a boy, and the moment he takes responsibility for the corpse, he starts to become a man.

And the trouble isn't over for Peter. Now he has had to use up all his father's inheritance. Has to give away all that wealth. What we don't yet realize is that he is unwittingly paying for all the wisdom he's going to receive a little way down the line.

In an odd way, there may be a reason no one recognizes the corpse. Because it's Peter's business now. The corpse *isn't* the same man they saw walking off into the fields the day before.

Because of Peter's willingness to take on this task of carrying the dead, he has ensured that the corpse becomes not a ghost but an ancestor. You may wish to think on that sentence. If we don't pay with all we know, if we don't accept the heavy task, then we likely live haunted lives not ancestral ones. You pay with what you learnt initially from a parent, and that is the heavy-coined price for now learning from the realm behind them.

So, seemingly within hours of leaving the father's home, Peter has taken on and honoured to the point of financial impoverishment a dead man. We can only wonder how he felt at the wake as the village wildly danced and drank and gobbled their way through every single penny of his inheritance. Thrilled, I'm sure. I'm really starting to like the guy.

Many therapists would encourage Peter to be free of the burden, to go live his best life without heft and responsibility, to even imply he was a little naïve to be giving away his entire inheritance for the sake of honouring the dead appropriately. What could that look like? It means not counting the cost when the giveaway comes, it means naming your hereditary influences and not pretending to be a genius touched only by god, it means tempering ambition so as to have a real, paid-in-full connection to what came before you. That you stand on the shoulders of giants.

And, of course, within hours, Peter has opened up an ancestral hotline. In a land of haunted people, Peter walks with an ancestor. A being of advisory insight, not wailing for reckoning or justice.

In every story in this book, there's bad deals and possession states. Terribly contemporary. What stands behind beautiful people seducing you to answer to bewildering and impossible questions? If you replace the mention of *questions* and replace it with *standards,* then we catch a glimpse. These berserk oligarchs of empty beauty who sit in their throne

71

rooms of Instagram and TikTok, starving and disorientating their subjects with expectations that can barely be met. And, like the Bewitched Princess, there's sometimes something older and savvier behind them, pulling on the strings. At its very worst, a spirit that is forever starving, insatiable for the entrancement of the human spirit. First Nations have sometimes called this presence *wetiko,* the Sufis the *nafs.*

I could fill many pages on the Mountain Spirit – sometimes called the Hostile Mountain Spirit. But it's foolish to attempt to reduce such an image; better to make a few associations and step back before it slips into the writer's very pen as revenge.

There's just something mean and cannibalistic out there. It moves in and out of communities as well as individuals. Some of us create better homes for it than others, lay down rotting meat and open bottles of cheap vodka so it feels comfy. Play death metal day and night, have internet porn on endless rotation. Very few Indigenous cultures I know of would claim these beings as completely contained within us, rather moving through us. It's an odd type of egotism to claim evil as entirely of a human's own making, any more than stating we created love, power or the gods.

There are places in this world that simply don't feel good, and traditionally we stay away from them, same with some people. Our hairs stand up and that's it, we back off. The Hostile Mountain Spirit is present.

The Mountain Spirit hates inventive thinking, loves to hypnotize and trap, and may have some hurt feelings that no one remembers his face anymore. He could be some abandoned and archaic god of sacrifice and blood. He may be the

Devil. But doesn't it serve him better not to be remembered? That way he can do his work in disguise and amnesia, but nasty things still get accomplished.

The first thing the Ancestor does for Peter is to give him wings. This is surprising. So far Peter has not seemed a winged kind of character; he has little ambition but is loyal to tradition and doing things correctly. Now the Ancestor has him flying (wonkily) up to listen in on the conversation between the princess and her lover. In those few seconds with the wings, Peter would have seen things he'd never seen before: distant forests, mountain peaks, maybe even the ocean. It's intoxicating. His wingspan, and therefore his life, are literally wider – the adventure is stretching him. The Ancestor is also educating him in some craftiness: if your life is on the line and a trap is being set, use every skill you have. A St George and the Serpent–type killing will not do. You have to be subtler than that.

When you take on something like the Mountain Spirit, you aren't going to see much to begin with. Keep back and out of sight. But over time you glimpse enough to get a summary: a terrible energy is directing the front-of-house attraction (the princess). Something beautiful is possessed by something very bad. Twice you earwig the question and are able to repeat the answer – the father's white horse alone in the stable, the father's sword – both images of status and male authority. Every time you visit, the cave grows brighter, in fact seems to be more advanced than expected; it's a mountain hall. And the previously empty altar fills with two very particular images, one of a fish and one of a wheel of fire. It's bewildering, but stay with it. By some persistence, some monstrous dynamic in our lives gradually has light shone on it.

This iconography starting to appear will direct many of us to two key developments in spiritual maturity, knowledge of soul and spirit. James Hillman wrote on the distinction masterfully, as have others. We have seen something of these attributes of the story already: in the corpse carrying and in the wings. To carry a corpse is a soulful activity. It equips us with knowledge of breathless labour, of limit, of aching shoulders, of how-many-more miles, of the end of life, of sorrowing, of abdicating advantage, of reduction in status, of watery and persistent depths. It deepens us. To carry wings equips us with knowledge of high and exciting views, the perils of the sun, sudden moves, brilliant insights, intoxicating possibility and the capacity to inspire. It stretches us. Most of us far prefer this second education.

The fish is an old sign of knowing watery, hidden places; the fiery wheel, an old sign of passion and promise. A fiery teacher lights up the room. A watery teacher lowers the lamp. A genius teacher is that rare soul that has strung the harp string of their character between both.

When you keep visiting the trouble, you start to see more. You move from the sometimes hallucinatory light of the moon to the brightness of sun. There is far less room for anything to hide in daylight. It's why, of course, all Devon forests are like Times Square once it gets dark.

And when you see enough, you have to move from stealth to action. You strike.

To carry a head into the negotiations is to display mastery over it. To break spells.

What fascinates me is the last scenes; of the Ancestor offering his advice concerning the wedding bath. The move from raven to dove to woman, from princess to queen.

Suddenly I don't see the story through Peter's or the Ancestor's eyes anymore. I see it through hers, the young queen's. Suddenly we see the necessity for her to meet Peter, of an energy able to stand between the force field of her and her lover. That, as long as she repeats these death-energy riddles, she remains perpetually removed from her true sovereign-hood. Just as Peter has gone from amiable loafer to focused warrior, she has gone from a shadowed dummy to a queen.

It is not for a leader to be possessed by raven or dove, but to have the maturity to let them speak when occasion befits. To negotiate the animal powers, not just be ridden by them. It often seems the task of our loved ones to point out when we are lacking the sobriety of the corvid or the settled vision of the dove. In their more troubling aspects, a raven leader longs for corpses to pick on, while a dove leader is unequipped to handle misrule.

There's far more going on here than this little commentary gives away, but that's for you to find out.

*Kicking the Robbers*
*Out of the House*

## To What Are You Returning?

You'll be pleased to know they all came back. The vigilers. Four days cradling their ear to the leafy navel of the world tree – which of course is the forest we work in. The weather threw them quite a bone by turning up a little heat after days of undecided splashes of grey and blue, a little Baba spit on their head here and there. There's a little tea, some breakfast, a dip into hot water and there the little chicks are. It's a proper morning-has-broken moment. They all seem mesmerized by each others' faces for a while, then bashful, even shy. Everyone looks so beautiful it's hard to hold their gaze. Conversations surge then dip, and me and the team prowl round with sticks, giving them a prod when they gaze too wistfully back into the forest. Because, despite the great weathering they have endured, once basic necessities have been accounted for – food, a scrub – the allure of the flickering dreaming of their forest spot beats its steady, courtly thump in their veins. Mostly they are in love with their place now, married to it, in fact.

There's a sense of bemused achievement at being defeated by something marvellous. It'll take years for them likely to be able to say much about what happened, but if you give it space and attention, things happen.

Whilst they rest and prepare to tell their story of the four days, we begin to look at the shape of the camp: billhooks, rope, tarps, firewood, kitchen area, fire pit, lanterns. It's vital that we leave the land so gently and lovingly it's as if we were never there. That we may, just possibly, have given something, rather than gobble, gobble, gobble.

It is always a marvel and privilege to hear the stories of the returning vigilers. That doesn't mean you are necessarily in the presence of master storytelling – that's not the emphasis. It means you see a human being in all their fragility trying to tell the truth, sometimes for the first time in their life. The philosophy of wilderness has had at them, the thinking of the wild.

It's in this rather vulnerable atmosphere we have to remind the vigilers that they are, in fact, only two-thirds of the way through the passage. That the most perilous stage is now awaiting them. The return. There's more malevolence, disorientation and possible hostility waiting for them there than ever was in that olde English forest. O pilgrim, the hard yards are now before you. The whole ceremony, thousands of years old, is now turned on its head in just a few years. The bush used to be the peril, not Santa Monica.

It could be that the return is actually when the wilderness vigil becomes the vision quest. It is certainly when – let it be so – we pray most fervently the wilderness epiphany becomes a village wisdom. That's no easy thing. Your average community usually aims to get the mystic on a spit as quickly as possible, rather than accommodate the crooked little insights the vigiler may return with. Toughen up, darlings, don't go easy.

It is time for our final story. About just the place the vigilers are returning to.

# THE SPYGLASS

*T*HERE *WAS ONCE A POOR*
hunter who lived with his mother in the mountains. Luckily he had uncanny skill with a bow, and
most of the time they ate well and their life had a
sweetness to it. They made much from what some
may regard as little.

But there was a day when nothing came to the
hunter, no animal laid down its life, so after a few
hours he was growing despondent. He didn't like
to see his mother without a hearty bowl of stew in
front of her, and a warming fire.

Suddenly he came across an eagle resting on a
rock. Resplendent. In a flash he had his arrow out
of his quiver and at his bow. But the eagle spoke, in
the high and powerful way that eagles do:

*'Spare my life and I will be useful to you. I will give
you a feather from my tail, and if you ever need help, burn
it and I will come to you.'*

An ally like that seemed far more useful than one
night's meal, so he accepted the arrangement and

walked on. Soon he came to a goat and prepared to catch it. But the goat spoke, in the trilling vibrato that goats have:

*'Spare my life and I will be useful to you. I will give you a hair from my beard, and if you ever need help, burn it and I will come to you.'*

The hunter was quick to realize he was collecting allies, not grub, and accepted the arrangement. But his gut ached, and he worried about his mother. It was now dark, so he crawled into a hollow tree and spent the night. Deep and strange his dreams.

In the morning he walked a long stretch to the sea, hoping for a fish. He waded out into the grey waves, managing to catch a fish that glistened exactly like gold. As he wrenched the fish out of the brine it spoke, in the gurgling and watery way that fish do:

*'Spare my life and I will be useful to you. I will give you a golden scale from my skin, and if you ever need help, burn it and I will come to you.'*

Though wobbly with fatigue, the hunter recognized that something startling was happening, and he placed the fish back in the salty swirl and accepted the scale.

Shivering and running up and down the beach to dry off, he spotted a red fox just up shore and again he creaked back his bow, though now half expecting the next scene, as the fox spoke, in the amused and cackling way that foxes do:

*'Spare my life and I will be useful to you. I will give you some fur from my tail, and if you ever need help, burn it and I will come to you.'*

So tired he could only nod, the hunter accepted
the fur, and the fox darted off into the brush. For
the rest of the day, the hunter walked – no birds,
no animals, grey skies, chill under his cloak. He
came to a settlement and visited a little hut on
its edge, smoke rising from the chimney. Inside
was the smallest, oldest woman he had ever seen.
Wrinkled like a currant she was, squatted down by
the fire, stroking her belly, gazing up and clearly
hungry. The hunter immediately reached into his
pocket and gave her a coin. A smile spread across
the moon of her face and she scuttled off to buy
some meat. Later they ate well and the hunter felt
finally refreshed, but he could feel the old woman
was disguising some sorrow. So he enquired. At
first she didn't want to disturb his eating, but after
some gentle nudging she spoke to her distress, let it
hover in the air between them.

She told him the kingdom had a harsh ruler with
many magics. That he had an odd entrancement on
his daughter. That he had given her a spyglass that
could see every single thing in the world. With this
device you could receive information in a fraction
of a second. Any man who would want to marry her
had to be nimble enough to evade her sight three
times. You showed your pedigree by disappearing.
By becoming nothing. Next to impossible for any
suitor, with the spyglass at her disposal. Any man
who failed was slaughtered. So far, ninety-nine
young men had died, including both the old

woman's sons — her winners-of-bread, her right arm, her sustenance.

Of course, the next day the hunter made his way to the ruler's compound. He was astonished at its opulence, the servants, the gathered wealth. He said he accepted the challenge, but on one condition: that he was allowed to hide not three times but four. It's something to negotiate under that kind of pressure, but the daughter accepted, whilst reminding him:

*'Your head is hanging by a thread!'*

Next morning, when the sun had barely opened his great hot eye, the hunter slipped away from the compound and burnt the eagle feather. Instantly the eagle was there, picked him up and carried the hunter to his nest, higher than the cloud line. He then spent the day covering the hunter with his wings.

Well, it was a hard thing for the daughter to locate. She worked over all the usual spots men hid in, and he wasn't there: not down a well, in the tavern, under his mother's apron, in an empty promise, not even in a hollow tree. Finally she spotted just a couple of hairs from the fur brim of his hat under the eagle's wing and shouted:

*'I found him! He did better than the rest, but I found him!'*

Next morning, when the sun was just starting to stir and contemplate the day's labours, the hunter slipped away from the compound and burnt the hair from the goat's beard. Instantly the goat was there, and the wild old thing carried the hunter to the very edge of the known and unknown world, dug a hole, nudged him in, and spent the day covering the hole with her furry, ample body.

Well, it was a hard thing for the daughter to locate. She had almost given up, almost started to gaze up behind the planets, when she spotted a little cloth from his jacket under the girth of the goat's belly and shouted:

*'I found him! He did better than the rest, but I found him!'*

Next morning, when the sun was stifling a yawn and assembling his rays, the hunter slipped away from the compound and burnt the golden scale of the fish. Instantly the fish was there, and the sea spirit placed the hunter in the mouth of a pike and took him far out over the green daggers of the sea, then deep down into its depths.

Well, it was a hard thing for the daughter to locate. She gazed on desert, swamp, forest and meadow and he was simply gone. She despaired until her mother prompted her to scan the deep sea. After some hours, she saw the pike open its mouth to swallow a fish and she saw, tucked down inside, the face of the hunter and shouted:

*'I found him! He did better than the rest, but I found him!'*

There was excitement in the chief's compound now as they felt the trap tightening, but also some barely whispered admiration for how far the hunter had managed to stretch the affair, his skills under pressure.

Next morning, when the sun was deciding to place one warm finger slow and curly over the top of the eastern hills, the hunter slipped away from the compound and burnt the fox's fur. Instantly the fox was there, and told him to relax and take a nap under a tree, that he'd fix everything. The fox then dug an underground tunnel to right underneath the daughter's chambers, halting just a few feet under her. Try as she might, wherever she aimed her spyglass, she couldn't find the hunter. Never would she think to look under her own feet.

That night when they met, she was so exasperated she asked for an extra day to locate him. With an easy smile he agreed, and the next morning burrowed along the tunnel and again spent the day right under her feet. As dusk came, in frustration she flung the spyglass against the wall, and suddenly a familial darkness flew out the window with it. Some healing had come.

Overnight her father slinked away into the forest, and the hunter became the husband of the princess of the kingdom. It was a merry time, and the hunter's mother was called over to the wedding. She danced for three hours with a man called Khabib. Contentment, for just as long as is proper, ruled the house. I told the stories. Oh, and I had a bottle of the finest cognac to share with you from the wedding, but a dark-eyed girl on a snorting white horse rode by and stole it from me, and I must give chase now to get it back!

A third story of leaving home. This time not through trauma or idle curiosity, but necessity. The hunter and his mother need to eat. Even as I write those words, my gut growls and I sniff the air for something roasting down in the belly of the cottage, down in the kitchen. We all know what it's like to be hungry, but rarely so acutely as the hunter and his mother. There's an urgency to the search when no animal gives itself to your bow and the woeful possibility arises that you may even have fallen out of favour with the archaic gods and goddesses of the hunt. Any hunter's kit is woven thick with prayers, spells and wondrous appeasements to the spirits of animals. And to be a hunter is defined by bringing back the stuff of life and death for others. No success, and soon your very identity will be brought into question. Thankfully for the hunter, this temporary stillness represents the moment before a rapid escalation of his relationship to the wild, rather than a miserable tapering off. His very title tells us this will be a story of pursuit, not steady, seeded growing. Both have the genius. But the story is whispering that we, too, have to remain light on our feet, an eye for what's moving up ahead in the bush, not to startle it.

And what an animal to encounter, the eagle. Hard not to think of it as top of the pile. Majestic, tough, deadly, imbued with strength and precision. And I'm not writing about eagle as totem but eagle as bird. Something you can watch and observe. Sometimes the greatest information a poet can glean is from simple observation – rather than immediately turning everything into a metaphor or allegory, fond as we are of both. Just let the bird be its birdness. Just look at it.

But then it does something that lets us know that another door has opened. The bird speaks. That's not normal. My instinct is that it's not even normal for the young hunter. Eagle negotiates. What could it mean to carry the feather of an eagle, to have a vast power like that at your back? I think if an eagle looked at me, it would look with anger, or sorrow. I feel he's looking at the hunter with invitation – one predator to another.

Then of course the same thing happens with the goat, the golden fish, the fox, but let's also not forget the night in a hollow tree. This whole series of encounters has a hinge in it: blessed night, dreaming in a circle, the rotten belly of a hollow tree. These animals are doing things that seem to belong in a dream as it is; they are pulling on some Eden-esque longing or some Inuit knowing. The animals are both the animals that the people of the region would recognize, but also magical inflammations: they rattle out human speak when the human is the right human that is standing in front of them.

So, as the hunter dreams, he falls ever deeper into the animistic arrangement he has now committed to. He is out on the taiga, or a Welsh hilltop, tucked in the dark of a South Dakota sweat lodge, submitting to the chewy mayhem of getting dreamt. People change after a night in a hollow tree, they change.

The hunter is now suitably infected by relationship to goat, eagle, fish and fox, and that rides alongside his instinctive protectiveness. It was concern for his mother that got him out hunting in the first place.

It is no surprise that he ends up in a hut at the edge of things with an old woman – he's gravitating to what is most natural to him. After all the animal negotiations, he's returning to a place where he can actually stop for a second and gather it all further into himself. He's spilling out all over the place at this stage.

Even so, he immediately gives money to the old woman and alleviates her suffering – in fact, is about to use all his new bartering to help her and the settlement. When we look at the old woman she is of course the old woman, but glance left for a second and you may see the iridescent power of the beauteous and jaw-droppingly ancient Earth Mother herself. No one quite knows what that is, but if you use your *wyrd* eye, you'll see something shift quickly. Like a bat or an owl. So, as from the beginning of the story, he is in service to the feminine, and the older, wizened and wiser variety. There's a reason animals come to his bow. Some ancient ceremony gets played out every time he walks the hills. They know whom he serves. And what a story she has for him.

A people tyrannized by a magical spyglass. In the midst of what feels like a very old story, we have advanced technology. Whilst the hunter is muttering with goats, the daughter of the ruler can see everything in the world, instantly. Everything is available to her.

If ever an image in an old tale spoke to me of right now – and you, of that I am certain – then this is it. There it is, right there. The shocking magic of the internet. And technology like that is always going to appear as if it's magic; that's part of its stun-value. The spyglass. In our cultural seizure of attention-grabbing madness, we'd hardly be difficult to spot. A second of scanning any number of social media devices and there we are, practically with a zip code tattooed across our face. And, of course, we have Google Earth for that, if needs be.

What's so extraordinary is not that you can be located on such a device, but that the very conditions that make you a sovereign are that you have to prove yourself invisible to it.

You have to conquer it.

Could we do that? We can barely put our phones on the table, let alone disappear.

This mind-boggling feat for the hunter is not easy. And if the hunter hadn't had the chutzpah to negotiate four not three tries, it would not have ended well for him. Four breaks the arrow tip of three, possesses a differing strength; it changes the dynamic that's proved so lethal for the people. If you ever find yourself the underdog, if you can change just one itsy-little detail of the negotiation, then you may just have room for a divine wind to enter. Try it.

To disappear. Not be dead, but be untraceable by the unblinking Eye of Sauron that is the spyglass. To do that very opposite of what modern society implores our youth to do: be *visible, visible, visible.* If losing your hands is collateral damage, so be it. If having a demonic lover is the result, well, chalk it up as experience. The main thing is to get out there and get seen – virtually at least.

The problem is until three minutes ago, no one bar a very few had to deal with the opinions of more than maybe thirty to forty people. We are now trained to fetishize dangling ourselves in front of maybe thirty or forty hundred, or thousand, maybe millions of people. This is a new problem for an entire generation of young people to filter. To bear the inhuman scrutiny of it. I can barely stand to tell you some of the stories arising from working with youth around this pressure. Self-harm to body dysmorphia to any number of ways to stretch yourself on the rack of public scrutiny.

Young boys so addicted to hard-core porn that sex with a girl seems 'vanilla' if it doesn't involve extreme violence and kink. There's even a phrase for how horrendously overstimulated sexual imagination seeks ever-growing darkness to stay interested: *blunting*. And before too long, even the genitals start to wither with the full-scale immersion. To hear of a teenager seeking Viagra is a desperately sad event. Everything is cranked-up, high-filtered, retina-rocking stimulation. Access to this entire world of demons and angels is on every smartphone in every kid's pocket.

Teenagers are meeting less and less in real time. Because nothing can compete with what they have in their hands. Teenage pregnancy is the lowest it's been for years (an upside), drinking is down, weed is up, conspiracies are up. The new normal is being more isolated than ever and being more connected than ever. A smartphone is not a benign device; it's an influencer with consuming ambitions.

If you don't find this terrifying, then you really haven't grasped the moment we're in. This is technology advancing far faster than the human mind. We are practically identical mentally (if not philosophically) to how we were fifty years ago. Do you think computers are?

We are not psychologically on the same page as where technology is taking us. We simply won't be able to catch up. Artificial intelligence is not a future threat, it's already arrived, designed to perfectly curate our dopamine addiction and desire to measure self-worth by hysterical visibility. I'm late to the party in seeing this, I admit, for two reasons: (1) I'm a terrible consumer in terms of the internet. They can't get much in front of me. (2) I've felt the very real benefits of the connectedness of the spyglass. As something of a hermit, it helps me reach out.

But I have to say, for future generations: *fuck this.* This is really, properly dangerous.

*Where has integrity gone?*
*Could the spyglass be rewired accordingly?*
*Can a humane technology be dreamed up?*
*How monstrous does this have to become?*

Helpless; it feels helpless. The spyglass seems to be in some horrendous waltz with climate emergency and conspiracy theories. Where once was earthy imagination, there now seems to be frantic fantasy. Elections get toughed out on social media in a hashtag frenzy. It is quite possible to stick to endless streams of posts that simply never contradict your view of reality.

And we have the audacity to call that community. That's not a community, that's a network. A community is wayward opinions bumping in and out of harmony with one another, not necessarily cooing over the hymn sheet.

I don't want to belabour this, because I'm assuming it's clear as day what I'm trying to say.

And wait a second.

In all this despair, there comes a response. Maybe not quite an answer, but a response.

Not from the eagle, not from the goat, not from the fish, but from the fox.

The single place the spyglass can't see is underneath you.

It can't see what's on your prayer mat.

Of course it's a fox, the one who sees everything a little different, that figures it out. Don't shelter in an eagle's nest, don't hide under a goat, don't dwell in the belly of a fish – go right and directly to the soul of the problem. Dig down and deep and you, too, will become like smoke. You, too, will disappear.

That prayer mat is your root system, your ancestral underpinning, your uninfluenced self, the residence of your daemon, your *ding! ding! ding!* boxing ring, your centre of sustained nobility and bullish decorum. Go there, my friends, go there. Blessed privacy awaits. The soul adores a beautiful door lovingly locked.

The soul is the one free-ranging, underground energy that the spyglass can't quite franchise.

Maybe in the end, the spyglass longs for one who will out-fox it. Maybe as the story suggests, it longs for defeat. That's naïve of me, but I'm suggesting it. We should remember, our prayer mat whispers, *know yourself*, so you don't need the spyglass to do it for you.

To be someone like the hunter is to be a breaker of spells. The counsel for us is clear:

In the name of everything that is good and holy in this world, understand the ground that technology *can't* bequeath you. If that is in place, it could even become a great ally, help you in all sorts of ancestral investigations. But such technology is ornamental to the task, not a root. It reverts to the role of tool, not deity. It becomes smaller, and of greater use.

If you don't know the ground underneath you, you could be a sitting duck. But if you do, you could offer informed resistance. Get wily, smoky, unpredictable.

When Google says *three,* you say *four.* Negotiate. We are not a resource. And our character and habits should not be relentlessly parcelled off and flogged to nefarious gatherers of personal data. But they already have. What to do?

Go sit quietly in wild places and see what wants to come talk to you. Get seasoned.

Get beautifully massacred by your totems.

Self-knowledge, mythic ground, attending to the grace, these are some of things that will provide pushback in such perilous times. Retune yourself. Pay attention to animals that talk, learn to stay your hand on occasion, be unexpectedly and repeatedly gracious. Be tough as hobnailed boots when you need to be. Know your worth.

In the end, you may become a leader of substance. That doesn't imply fame. You may bring a nimble infusion of love and courage into the world. Doesn't matter your age, colour or where you are on the spectrum of anything. Some people are wary of inflammatory ideas like that, and I understand why. A little grandiose. I don't respect the caution but I understand it.

But.

If I'd listened to every half-lived caution like that, I never would have written a word, and if you are still reading, there's a chance you may be just as ornery as me.

In the end, if you don't know your ground, you won't be able to know what truth feels like anymore. You just won't.

There'll be no smoke hole, only the spyglass.

Take courage.

I say it again:

*Kick the robbers out of the house.*

*Take your imagination back.*

# THE STORIES

# THE HANDLESS
# MAIDEN

*T*HERE ONCE WAS A MILLER,
his wife and their daughter. There'd been a time
when life had been grand, wealth had flowed like
milk and the wheel of the mill had merrily creaked.
But all that was long ago. On the day our story
begins, the miller was a mile from home, out in
the dark wood. It was dusk, and he was gathering
kindling for the fire. In his scratching for survival,
he didn't notice he'd caught someone's attention.
From behind a tree appeared a man, a very small
man, pale skin, the brim of a hat covering much of
his face. The watcher spoke:

*'Miller, miller, miller. It pains me to see you in this
situation. Truly it does. I remember what good you've done
in the village, the parties you've held, the drinks you've
poured, the poor you've aided. And to see you here today,
scavenging in the grasses for twigs. It's degrading, especially
for a man of such status. I can't bear it, and I can't
imagine how you must feel about it.'*

The miller glanced up for a second and let the cooing land on him. He blinked rapidly in the disappearing light, and the small man continued:

'As a fellow of the wood, I have magic in me. Powerful magic. I'll tell you what, dear miller. As your biggest supporter, let me endorse you. I am going to reverse your bad fortune. From this moment on, anything you desire you can have. Just think it and it's there. The good times are coming back. You and your family will be rich again.'

He now had the miller's full attention, and he piped up:

*'I love this idea. Gods I do. But what would you want in return? You must want something.'*

At this, the fellow of the wood looked thoughtful, as if such a thing hadn't occurred to him.

'Well, for the sheer etiquette of the spell, I suppose I should take some trinket. It is endless wealth I'm giving you, after all. I tell you what: in exchange for all those riches, I will take everything that is behind your hovel at this moment.'

The miller thought for a second: all that was there was an apple tree. Nothing of any significance. I mean, this was the deal of his life.

'Absolutely. I agree. Whatever is behind the home at this moment, you may have.'

At this, a shriek came from the pale man, which he quickly muffled.

'Oh, good for you, *good for you.* I'm delighted to have helped. My spell will be immediate, from

this moment, wealth is running back towards you.
Scampering, singing, wending its way towards you.
I will come next Thursday, to give you a few days
to think about the deal, and exactly whom you may
have struck it with.'

And with that, he slipped back into the trees, an
odd perfume remaining.

It was now almost entirely dark.

Even as he walked back to his home, in the
gloom he could see his wife coming towards him,
walking fast over the fields, her rough, itchy skirt
replaced by an elegant dress, pearls at her neck.

'Husband! Husband! It's a miracle. The kitchen
is filled with hocks of ham, strings of onions and
garlic, lamb, freshly baked bread, cream cakes and
good wine in the cellar. There are paintings hanging
on the walls, stacked wood by the fire, a fine new
jacket and waistcoat for you all laid out on the bed.
How could this happen?'

'Ah, details, details. Now, where is our daughter,
so she may share in our good fortune?'

'Why, husband, how could you even ask that
question?

'She's where she always is.'

*Behind the house*

*Under the apple tree*

*Sweeping back and forth*

It was then, and only then, did the miller realize
the deal he'd struck, and quite whom he'd struck
it with.

The daughter took the news soberly, almost
as if she expected it. Even as the affluence came
raining down, she seemed to withdraw into herself.
Amongst all the frivolity, she was focused on
something no one else could quite see. On the day
the man of the wood arrived to collect, she bathed,
put on a white dress, and drew a chalk circle around
her. She stood calmly at the circle's centre, and
gazed levelly at him.

It was the strangest thing. No matter how he
tried, he could not enter the circle. He dodged
this way and even leapt frantically in the air, but
he simply could not enter her circle. After twenty
minutes he was spent.

'Miller,' he wheezed, 'this was not the
arrangement. Not the deal at all. She's too clean,
too pristine, too contained. I can't bend her. I will
return in one week's time and expect her muddied
by this world: grimy, bedraggled, broken even. I'll
have no problem whisking her off then.'

Feeling the unmentioned threat of consequence,
the miller forbade his daughter to bathe, removed
the chalk, encouraged her to rub mud on her skin,
weave twigs and ivy in her hair, to stink. He and
his wife took no pleasure in this, but were simply
terrified. This is called being in way over your head.

The day came and shuffling down from the
treeline came the pale man with the hat covering
half his face. He initially looked pleased at the
state of the girl, but as he walked towards her, she

started to cry, to really weep. Not tears of fear, but of grief. She wept as we weep once or twice in our life. Tears that carry amniotic fluid and sea salt and the dreams of the sirens in them. Tears that push all before them, that hurl truth, sorrow and defiance into this world, all at once. As she wept, she wiped the tears over her bruised and muddied body. As the tears made tracks, her skin started to gleam. Clean and bright again.

Oh, and so moon bright it was, it was as if that chalk circle had returned. For the second time, the creature could not get his hands on the girl.

'Miller,' he snarled, 'this was not our arrangement. I wanted the smear of the world on her, depressed and filthy. She's not depressed, she's grieving. It's the hands. It's her hands that reach out towards joy and fulfilment, that wiped her body clean with those tears. Get rid of them. Take a silver axe and cut her hands off. You must do it. And if you don't, not only will the wealth disappear, I will bring a killing blight to the village, and your name will be ruined. This is your very last chance.'

As he angrily walked away, the daughter turned to the miller and said this:

*You were my gatekeeper,*
*And you let in the wolf.*

'Do it.'

The silver axe was gathered, and with all his might, the miller brought the axe down on his daughter's wrists.

A week later the being loped from the woods a third time. He saw the Handless Maiden's stumps and rejoiced. He saw the destroyed miller, the emaciated mother, and he rejoiced. He peered and sniffed and spat on the ground. And for a second time she started to weep, and it was as if those tears had an agency of their own, they moved around the girl's body without even the use of hands; like lively rivers, surging creeks, sparkling streams. There were salmon in those tears, deep-sea secrets, the defiance of the shipwrecked. The tears washed her clean again, top to bottom, resplendent.

She stuck her chin up. *Fuck you.*

Well, even fellows from the woods seem to know you have to give up on the third attempt. It's just a thing.

Muttering curses we can't quite decipher, he turned and shuffled across the darkening. An odd detail: the strangest thing was that the wealth continued, the deal didn't break. And no curse on the house. Except maybe the worst.

One night, whilst her parents feasted, the Handless Maiden slipped away into the dark forest.

*You were my gatekeeper,*
*And you let in the wolf.*

When an old story says she wandered for four days in the forest, that could be four months or years. And wander she did. In circles mostly. There were no fellow travellers, no cheery firesides, no tales of encouragement and fortitude. The only trail she encountered was the one she made by walking it. When she slept, her dreams were sour and disorientating; when she woke, she rarely knew where she was. All streams were sluggish, water brackish, and it's hard to hunt when you have no hands. Occasionally a bird would leave a little something to chew on. She'd gratefully gobble it down, belly tight and diminished, stuck to spine like a tight little drum. The forest had at her, from every direction. After a time you'd be hard-pressed to tell if she was a woman, a spirit of the forest, a wolf, so altered was she. The trunks of the trees were like prison bars, and she longed for a wide, open view. But, like her father the miller, she had to keep her eyes close to the ground, looking for kindling. It was a diminished world she peered out at.

For a long time, it stayed like this, exactly like this.

One night she was suddenly at the other side of the forest. There'd been no warning, no preamble, but there she was. The trees were behind her, and in the night sky was a vast yellow moon, full as the face of a coin. Underneath the moon was a castle, an orchard and, surrounding both, a moat. She could see the trees were swollen with apples and pears, even from a distance. Oh, she was desirous of such fruit. It made her skip foot to calloused foot, imagining their taste. Even as she had the sensation, she felt cautious to leave the shelter of the trees. So strange – all she'd done was fantasize about leaving, and now she hesitated. But in the end, both hunger and curiosity prevailed and she stalked her way down to the moat.

They say that the waters of the moat parted for her, a Red Sea moment. They say that trees shuffled forward in the dark earth, such was their ambition to feed her. They say she reached up with her bandaged stumps and pulled down a pear. When she'd consumed it, caution moved through her again and she scuttled back to the treeline. Not into its depths but at the edge of both the royal lands and the forest.

She'd been spotted, glimpsed by a gardener who worked by the moon, not the sun. He'd seen the strange unfolding. He wondered at it all, and next day reported it to the king, a young man who loved unusual stories. The king had the habit of many sovereigns, which was to count his fruit every morning, and he'd noticed one was missing. Well, this was the gardener's moment, so he told the story with full aplomb, and the two of them elected to go back to the orchard that very night and see if she returned.

She did, and the king asked her, gently and with full curiosity, quite who or what she was: a woman, a spirit of the forest, a wolf? She thought on it, chewed on it, bent her soul to it and replied:

*'I'm not sure. I've spent so very long in the forest I just don't know anymore.'*

That's the response of a grown woman.

Some say that the king fell in love with the Handless Maiden despite the wild hair, wolfish stance, circling crows. I tell you that's nonsense. The king fell in love with her *because* of the wild hair, wolfish stance, circling crows. He thought she was the most fascinating creature he'd ever met.

The king offered her quarters in the castle, plenty of space to rest and gather herself, and she accepted. She could see the forest from her bedroom window and felt sufficiently recovered to enjoy this next stage in her journey. Journey to quite what, she had no idea. It won't surprise you that every day, the lovestruck young king would take a little tea to her door, maybe some musicians, good food. He adored her. He started to work on poetry of varying quality, and one day his heart forced him to make his big gesture, standing before her and saying:

*In your bright braided tresses*
*There is a flock of songbirds,*
*Your eyes are like keen crystal,*
*Set in a ring.*

*Your cheek is red like the coal of a fire,*
*And your mouth speaks old words,*
*Like the roar of the waterfall.*

*You are whiter than the swan on the pool,*
*More tuneful than the fiddle,*
*You are a ship on a mistless wave.*

*When I saw you,*
*I thought the moon herself had*
*Fallen into a bed of wild flowers*

*And was singing an old song*
*I had waited my whole life*
*To hear.*

She fell ardently into the fur of his words, and
a love affair began. The castle was a place of fresh,
sparky life and laughter, the king's mother adored
the young woman and it wasn't too long before a
marriage proposal spilled from the mouth of the
king. She accepted.

As a wedding gift, her husband gave the
Handless Maiden the one thing she clearly did not
have – a pair of hands, painstakingly crafted from
silver – meant quite sincerely. She felt his good
will, but rarely wore them.

After a time she felt different: expanded,
assaulted, blessed. She was pregnant.

She would sit by the fire with her husband, deerhounds at their feet as they speculated on this new life
growing inside her. They tried out baby names and
giggled into the small hours. So deep the bliss, it was
a vile wrench when the king was called to war at the
edge of the kingdom. It was his first war, and the eyes
of his people were on him to prove himself. He had
to lead from the front. He left with heavy heart and
the condition that if his wife were to give birth in his
absence, the castle was to send their speediest rider to
him to relay the news to wherever he may be fighting.

Though she missed her husband, the pregnancy
went well and the Handless Maiden gave birth to a

cherubic little boy. Happy hands, happy feet, merry little face, ready for mischief. The speediest rider was sent for and he sped out over the drawbridge, seeking the king.

After a time, it just so happened the rider found himself back in the woods where our story began. And the strangest thing came over him. A fatigue, a walloping exhaustion, a deep, mysterious drowsiness. He leant up against an oak and rested, his horse munching grass. He was barely conscious – almost dreaming – when a small, pale man with a large hat slipped out from behind a tree and spoke:

*'Speedy rider. You will tell the king an abomination has occurred. That the queen has not given birth to either a boy or a girl, but a dog, a terrible hound. That's what you get when you marry a woman of the forest. Tell him this news.'*

The speedy rider woke from his trance, took in the message and rode like the devil to the tent of the king. The king urgently received the rider and listened to the message intently. He grew quiet and looked out over the battlefield, gazing at the piles of dead warriors who would never see their families or home again. He chewed hard on his thinking. Finally he turned:

*'Though this is not the news I expected, still I welcome it. Whatever has come from my wife's womb will be loved by me, whatever its shape. Tell my beloved that I am humbled that she is so delightfully full of surprises, that I will be back the moment I can, and that my heart bangs wild under my breastplate with joy.'*

After some venison and beer, the rider rode back
over the heath and into the forest with the message,
wondering at the maturity of the king. Ah, but
after a time, a weariness came over him, didn't it?
A need to rest by the old oak tree, under its lush
bough. His horse munching grass, he barely noticed
when a small, pale man with a large hat slipped out
from behind the very tree he was slumped against:

*'Speedy rider. You will tell the queen mother that he is
appalled that such a demonic abomination has occurred,
that he will not suffer it to live, nor his witch wife. That he
expects the heart and tongue of his wife presented to him on
a plate on his return from war. Tell her this news.'*

The speedy rider woke from his trance and rode
like the devil to the castle of the queen mother.
The queen mother heard the message and grew
quiet, looking out of the window a time before
she spoke.

'It is clear that the brutality of war has sent my
child utterly mad. This is ludicrous and nothing
of the sort is going to take place. However, what is
clear is my daughter-in-law and my grandson are no
longer safe. Please summon them.'

When they were all gathered together, the queen
mother told the Handless Maiden a hard thing. That
she and her son would have to venture back out into
the forest until this horrible episode was cleared up
and it was safe for her to return. At this, the maiden
wept, shuddered and grew pale at the thought. But
her mother-in-law was sage and kind, saying:

*'I know, I know. But I tell you this. The dark forest is
never quite the same the second time around. Believe me.
It isn't and it won't be. Take courage, gather yourself, and
you will surprise yourself. But for now, it is urgent that
you leave.'*

Early the next morning, a hat concealing most of
her face, the maiden and her child slipped into the
treeline and disappeared.

*Never quite the same the second time.*

Towards the end of the day, the maiden did
indeed see something she'd never set eyes on before
in the forest: a friendly trail of smoke. Someone
was out here too. Someone else was surviving in
this environment. She followed the smoke, baby in
her arms, till she saw its source. It was coming from
the chimney of a rustic cottage.

She could hear rascal laughter, cheery singing,
so she peered through the window. She could
see women, many women, of all ages. Some
were gathered by the fire, some knitting, some
cooking, gossiping – the mood seemed wonderful.
They spotted her peering in, and the door was
swiftly opened. She was emphatically gathered in,
with all cooing over the moon-faced babe. From
the moment she sat with them and powerfully
recounted her story, it was clear she had found a
new home, in the exact place that she was most
terrified to go to. These stalwart women were
called the Wood Sisters, and gathered under their
shawls, they had a great understanding of the inner

rhythms of the forest. Things grow in a cottage like that, things get better, even cautiously recover.

*And a great wonder happened*
*A joy beyond reckoning*

She started to grow her hands back. Bit by bit. It could have been the first time she defended her child or stood naked in the storm, or wrestled a root from the soil, but she started to heal, right there. Not as a solitary hero fighting a dragon, but right there in the fine company of the Wood Sisters. And it is a powerful thing for a young lad to grow with a cackling flank of jubilant aunties around him. For some years it continued like that, lively and restorative, but I cannot tell you that the maiden did not wonder what had happened to her husband. I cannot tell you she didn't gaze out at dusk, make a bed for her sorrow.

And what of her husband? When he returned, jubilant and expectant to meet his wife and dog-child, he was stricken with terror when presented with the heart and tongue on the plate (those of a doe). When his mother saw that there must have been subterfuge in the messaging back and forth, she told her son everything:

*'And now she and your boy are out there in the forest. It is up to you to find them. I thought they had to go there for their own protection. But now I wonder if it is indeed you who needs to go there. I'd always wondered on the imbalance of forest knowledge between you and your dear wife. It is your turn for the great wandering, my dear son, and I wish you wisdom and protection as you go.'*

Having not even removed his mud-caked cloak, his sword and belt, the king turned from his mother and rode wearily alone into the forest. He did not behold the trail of smoke on the first day, or the second, or the third. He beheld sodden flanks of branch and leaf, drizzling mists, tracks that led nowhere. He beheld nightmares, blustering and endless snowstorms, ravenous black bears and any number of sorrows hanging on him from the battlefield. A year turned into two into three and onwards. After seven years, his hair and beard fell to his waist, hands nicked and scarred, barely recognizable from the buoyant young sovereign of years past. There was a weight to him, a seriousness. And still he searched, way past the time when most of us would have retired from such a hopeless cause.

*But comes a day comes a day comes a day*
*When he saw the blue smoke*
*A cottage, the sound of laughter and singing*

Male voices, low and jovial, of all ages. He caught the scent of cherry tobacco and thought he recognized a folk song. He weakly knocked on the door – just a tap – and it swung open. He was gleefully gathered in by the men, sat by the fire, a bowl of elk stew and crusty buttered bread, a pint of dark beer. Paradise comes in many forms. And he asked:

'Have you heard of a woman and child, coming this way?'

111

'Oh, we have, we have. We are the Wood Brothers, and they live with the women we adore, the Wood Sisters, just a mile or so away.'

Word was speedily sent to the women's cottage, and by the end of day, the men could hear the women approaching, singing and dancing, all dressed top to toe, abundant in their finery. The men had scrubbed up well and encouraged each other to be bold in the face of the magnificence of the women. At some point, the tones of the women and the men's singing joined into something quite wonderful. And the Woman Who Grew Her Own Hands Back was reunited with the Man of the Deep Places.

For a moment, a veil was held between them, by the oldest woman and oldest man, and then it was dropped.

*And for just a second, they saw each other as God sees them.*

Just a second, but that beholding can be long enough to sustain a marriage when the road is long, awfully twisty and occasionally more than a little mad.

If there was any joy left to attain in the king's heart, he just about exploded when he looked down and saw his lad holding on to his belt, smiling up at him. He gathered him up weeping, then gazed in wonder at his wife's beautiful, restored hands. She smiled:

*'I'll tell you about them later.'*

Of course there was then days of feasting, and everyone fell in love with each other, even the long married. It was a long and happy life for our three.

And how do we know this story at all?

The son of the two of them became a storyteller, and wandered the courts and firesides of old Europe telling the story of a woman who grew her own hands back and a father who never gave up. And he told someone, who told someone else, who told someone else, and I find myself telling the story to you here today.

And I ask you:

*What are you going to do with it?*

# THE BEWITCHED
# PRINCESS

*T*HERE WAS ONCE A LAD CALLED
Peter. Not a king or a lord, just a man from a hut
that he lived in with his father. Peter was bored. He
didn't have any great plan, just a sense that he needed
to get out into the world, see a few things. He spoke
to his father who understood such a longing, and the
old man gave him his inheritance and watched his
son take the lonely road from their settlement.

It was thirty pieces of silver that Peter now had
in his pocket. He loved to feel the weight of them,
the bulge. More money than he'd ever seen. That
early morning, he walked beyond the world he knew
and out towards whatever his destiny was. He may
have fantasized about meeting a lover, or wrestling
a dragon, but he had no wondering at all for what
actually transpired. He came across a corpse lying
by the side of the road. Maybe a man like him, from
humble beginnings. He stared at the body for a bit,
noticed the crows starting to circle, picked up the

body and staggered with it to the next village. He called out to the villagers that this man deserved a proper burial, but no one seemed to recognize him. Peter had seen this kind of thing before. He took out his purse of silver and offered to pay for the funeral. It was the funniest thing – a miracle – suddenly the entire village remembered the dead man – in fact, remembered him going out to work the fields just that morning. Remembered they loved him, and if Peter just relinquished his purse, they'd see to the funeral. Well Peter did, and it was quite the send-off, with an extended and bounteous wake.

The next day, Peter set off on the road out of town, penniless and a little hungover. After a time, a man walked out from a field in the early-morning mist and started keeping step with him. Peter barely looked to his left, as he knew it was the dead man.

Some hours into hard walking and unable to shake his new companion, Peter arrived at a town. He'd rarely seen a settlement that big, and its appearance was even more unsettling. Everything was black. The tavern sign was black, the ice on the pond was black, even the pale children wore black clothes. A shroud had been flung over the place.

When he asked about it, Peter was told that town was in mourning; that their princess was bewitched by a mountain spirit who lived up behind the houses. That he was her lover and had possessed her. He used her as a rag doll for his desire, which was the death of young men. The way that was achieved was like this: the princess would give three riddles to potential suitors; if they could answer, none of them were executed. Nine of the brightest men in the area were already dead. You went into the princess's castle and never came out. Only the mountain spirit knew the answers to these strange questions that were not really riddles at all, as you'd never be able to guess them.

High stakes indeed, for the hand of the princess.

Even so, Peter resolved to try. With his ghostly companion, he was offered a room at the castle, and then over the following three days the riddles would be delivered. That night, Peter's companion beckoned him over to the window. They saw the princess floating up towards the mountain and her terrible lover. Over the fields she floated, over the swaying pines she floated, over the silvery streams she floated, above it all, high in the dank air.

The dead man produced from somewhere a set of leathery wings that he fitted with straps to Peter and told him to follow. Precariously, Peter set out. High up on the glowering mountain was the entrance to a cave. Peter saw the princess alight and walk into its darkness. A minute or two later, he landed and tentatively followed. It was a gloomy night, just a few stars brocading the way above him. He crept past an altar, but couldn't make out what was displayed on it.

He saw a vigorous-looking man with a long white beard seize the princess and run his hands

all over her. She in turn told him about the arrival
of Peter, and that she needed three new riddles if
they were to kill another young man. The mountain
spirit liked this, and stroked his beard:

*'Think of your father's white horse, all alone in the
stable. Tell the suitor to guess what you are thinking.'*

With that, the spirit's eyes flared up red and
ravenous:

*'The more death you bring me, the more blood you bring
me, the closer we are.'*

What a terrible covenant between lovers.

The next day, Peter went to see the princess.
She was all in black, pale and quiet, as if she had a
secret. She asked him the riddle that is not really a
riddle at all:

*'What am I thinking of?'*

*'You are thinking of your father's white horse, all alone
in the stable.'*

It was as if a funeral bell had struck. She shuddered, and really looked at him for the first time.
She bade him return tomorrow.

That night from his window, he saw her float
up towards the mountain and her terrible lover.
Over the dreams of the people she floated, over the
responsibilities of her role she floated, over even
her identity as a woman she floated. Into the arms
of her lover in the dark of his cave.

Peter's wings were strapped on by his dead
companion, and he flew upwards, stronger this
time, following the princess. He noticed the cave

was a touch brighter, the moon was growing and
was making it easier to see. He could just about tell
that it was not even really a cave but a large hall,
deep in the mountain. This time on the altar he
could see there was a fish. The princess ran to her
lover and he seized her with his hot hands. She told
him what had transpired with Peter, and he quickly
shot back with the next riddle:

*'Think of your father's sword. Tell the suitor to guess
what you are thinking.'*

Of course, the next day Peter had the answer to
the riddle.

The third night he flew up to the mountain
spirit's hall, it wasn't just moonlight that had
started to illuminate the area but actually sunlight.
He could see that on the altar next to the fish was a
wheel of fire, turning and sparking bright. Realizing
he could be spotted, he hid behind the stone shrine
and peered out. Uncomfortably blinking in the
rapidly lightening hall, the spirit hissed when he
heard the news that Peter had guessed the second
riddle. With that, he tugged on his beard, his eyes
flashed hot and weird, and he suddenly looked far,
far older than he had before:

*'Think of my face. No human can remember something
so ancient. Tell the suitor to guess what you are thinking.'*

After that the two lovers were together awhile,
and then she left, walking by Peter sheltering
behind the altar of the fiery wheel and the fish.
When he saw her step into the darkness and float

towards the castle, Peter came out from what was
left of the shadows and swiftly decapitated the
mountain spirit, placing his furious, ancient head
in his bag and flying down on those wings the dead
man had given him, stronger than ever now.

The next day he was summoned to the princess,
and she gave the third and final riddle.

*'What am I thinking of?'*

*'You are thinking of exactly this.'*

And with that, he rolled the head of her terrible
lover out of his bag to her feet.

She rolled and she rocked, gnashed and wailed,
but some awful energy passed from her body.
When she had recovered, she did indeed accept
the hand of Peter in marriage. Soon, the shroud
was being lifted off the town, the tavern sign was
repainted, the ice melted on the pond, the children
wore bright colours, the deep silence of the place
was replaced by music and chatter, townsfolk were
out on the streets again. What a celebration this
would be! Just before the wedding night, the dead
companion came to Peter:

*'The sweetest thing you can give your wife is this.*
*Prepare her a bath before the two of you make love. When*
*the water touches her, she will become a raven and attempt*
*to fly out the window. Catch the raven and place it back*
*in the bath. When the water touches her, she will become a*
*dove and attempt to fly out the window. Catch the dove and*
*place it back in the bath. After these animal shapes, you will*
*behold your beloved not as a princess anymore, but as a*

*queen. This is my last piece of guidance. From tomorrow, I will have disappeared.'*

The night transpired just as the companion advised, and in the morning, when Peter searched for him, he was gone. From that day forth, the people had a queen with the battle insight of a raven, the gentleness of a dove, and free from all enchantments.

# THE SPYGLASS

*T*HERE WAS ONCE A POOR
hunter who lived with his mother in the mountains. Luckily he had uncanny skill with a bow, and
most of the time they ate well and their life had a
sweetness to it. They made much from what some
may regard as little.

But there was a day when nothing came to the
hunter, no animal laid down its life, so after a few
hours he was growing despondent. He didn't like
to see his mother without a hearty bowl of stew in
front of her, and a warming fire.

Suddenly he came across an eagle resting on a
rock. Resplendent. In a flash he had his arrow out
of his quiver and at his bow. But the eagle spoke, in
the high and powerful way that eagles do:

*'Spare my life and I will be useful to you. I will give
you a feather from my tail, and if you ever need help, burn
it and I will come to you.'*

An ally like that seemed far more useful than one
night's meal, so he accepted the arrangement and

walked on. Soon he came to a goat and prepared to catch it. But the goat spoke, in the trilling vibrato that goats have:

*'Spare my life and I will be useful to you. I will give you a hair from my beard, and if you ever need help, burn it and I will come to you.'*

The hunter was quick to realize he was collecting allies, not grub, and accepted the arrangement. But his gut ached, and he worried about his mother. It was now dark, so he crawled into a hollow tree and spent the night. Deep and strange his dreams.

In the morning he walked a long stretch to the sea, hoping for a fish. He waded out into the grey waves, managing to catch a fish that glistened exactly like gold. As he wrenched the fish out of the brine it spoke, in the gurgling and watery way that fish do:

*'Spare my life and I will be useful to you. I will give you a golden scale from my skin, and if you ever need help, burn it and I will come to you.'*

Though wobbly with fatigue, the hunter recognized that something startling was happening, and he placed the fish back in the salty swirl and accepted the scale.

Shivering and running up and down the beach to dry off, he spotted a red fox just up shore and again he creaked back his bow, though now half expecting the next scene, as the fox spoke, in the amused and cackling way that foxes do:

*'Spare my life and I will be useful to you. I will give you some fur from my tail, and if you ever need help, burn it and I will come to you.'*

So tired he could only nod, the hunter accepted the fur, and the fox darted off into the brush. For the rest of the day, the hunter walked – no birds, no animals, grey skies, chill under his cloak. He came to a settlement and visited a little hut on its edge, smoke rising from the chimney. Inside was the smallest, oldest woman he had ever seen. Wrinkled like a currant she was, squatted down by the fire, stroking her belly, gazing up and clearly hungry. The hunter immediately reached into his pocket and gave her a coin. A smile spread across the moon of her face and she scuttled off to buy some meat. Later they ate well and the hunter felt finally refreshed, but he could feel the old woman was disguising some sorrow. So he enquired. At first she didn't want to disturb his eating, but after some gentle nudging she spoke to her distress, let it hover in the air between them.

She told him the kingdom had a harsh ruler with many magics. That he had an odd entrancement on his daughter. That he had given her a spyglass that could see every single thing in the world. With this device you could receive information in a fraction of a second. Any man who would want to marry her had to be nimble enough to evade her sight three times. You showed your pedigree by disappearing. By becoming nothing. Next to impossible for any suitor, with the spyglass at her disposal. Any man who failed was slaughtered. So far, ninety-nine young men had died, including both the old woman's sons – her winners-of-bread, her right arm, her sustenance.

Of course, the next day the hunter made his way to the ruler's compound. He was astonished at its opulence, the servants, the gathered wealth. He said he accepted the challenge, but on one condition: that he was allowed to hide not three times but four. It's something to negotiate under that kind of pressure, but the daughter accepted, whilst reminding him:

*'Your head is hanging by a thread!'*

Next morning, when the sun had barely opened his great hot eye, the hunter slipped away from the compound and burnt the eagle feather. Instantly the eagle was there, picked him up and carried the hunter to his nest, higher than the cloud line. He then spent the day covering the hunter with his wings.

Well, it was a hard thing for the daughter to locate. She worked over all the usual spots men hid in, and he wasn't there: not down a well, in the tavern, under his mother's apron, in an empty promise, not even in a hollow tree. Finally she spotted just a couple of hairs from the fur brim of his hat under the eagle's wing and shouted:

*'I found him! He did better than the rest, but I found him!'*

Next morning, when the sun was just starting to stir and contemplate the day's labours, the hunter slipped away from the compound and burnt the hair from the goat's beard. Instantly the goat was there, and the wild old thing carried the hunter to the very edge of the known and unknown world, dug a hole, nudged him in, and spent the day covering the hole with her furry, ample body.

Well, it was a hard thing for the daughter to locate. She had almost given up, almost started to gaze up behind the planets, when she spotted a little cloth from his jacket under the girth of the goat's belly and shouted:

*'I found him! He did better than the rest, but I found him!'*

Next morning, when the sun was stifling a yawn and assembling his rays, the hunter slipped away from the compound and burnt the golden scale of the fish. Instantly the fish was there, and the sea spirit placed the hunter in the mouth of a pike and took him far out over the green daggers of the sea, then deep down into its depths.

Well, it was a hard thing for the daughter to locate. She gazed on desert, swamp, forest and meadow and he was simply gone. She despaired until her mother prompted her to scan the deep sea. After some hours, she saw the pike open its mouth to swallow a fish and she saw, tucked down inside, the face of the hunter and shouted:

*'I found him! He did better than the rest, but I found him!'*

There was excitement in the chief's compound now as they felt the trap tightening, but also some barely whispered admiration for how far the hunter had managed to stretch the affair, his skills under pressure.

Next morning, when the sun was deciding to place one warm finger slow and curly over the top of the eastern hills, the hunter slipped away from the compound and burnt the fox's fur. Instantly the fox was there, and told him to relax and take a nap under a tree, that he'd fix everything. The fox then dug an underground tunnel to right underneath the daughter's chambers, halting just a few feet under her. Try as she might, wherever she aimed her spyglass, she couldn't find the hunter. Never would she think to look under her own feet.

That night when they met, she was so exasperated she asked for an extra day to locate him. With an easy smile he agreed, and the next morning burrowed along the tunnel and again spent the day right under her feet. As dusk came, in frustration she flung the spyglass against the wall, and suddenly a familial darkness flew out the window with it. Some healing had come.

Overnight her father slinked away into the forest, and the hunter became the husband of the princess of the kingdom. It was a merry time, and the hunter's mother was called over to the wedding. She danced for three hours with a man called Khabib. Contentment, for just as long as is proper, ruled the house. I told the stories. Oh, and I had a bottle of the finest cognac to share with you from the wedding, but a dark-eyed girl on a snorting white horse rode by and stole it from me, and I must give chase now to get it back!

# ACKNOWLEDGEMENTS

Warmest thanks to *Emergence* magazine for printing "Keeping the Smoke Hole Open" at the beginning of lockdown. You greatly assisted its impact. I also want to thank the anthropologist Dr Carla Stang for any number of collaborations, but specifically the Wedding the Wild gathering of 2017. We dreamed up the title together, and something very near that phrase and sentiment is mentioned within these pages. Good cheer. I'm grateful to my publisher Chelsea Green and especially my editor Muna Reyal for making this such an enjoyable experience. Finally to my daughter, Dulcie Shaw. Our endless chats, adventures and feasts are my delight. I'm so very proud of you.

# ABOUT THE AUTHOR

Dr Martin Shaw is an acclaimed teacher of myth. Author of the award-winning Mythteller Trilogy (*A Branch from the Lightning Tree, Snowy Tower, Scatterlings*), he founded the Oral Tradition and Mythic Life courses at Stanford University and is director of the Westcountry School of Myth in the United Kingdom.

He has introduced thousands of people to mythology and how it penetrates modern life. For twenty years, Shaw has been a wilderness rites of passage guide, working with at-risk youth, those who are unwell, returning veterans as well as many women and men seeking a deeper life.

His translations of Gaelic poetry and folklore (with Tony Hoagland) have been published in *Orion Magazine, Poetry International, Kenyon Review, Poetry* magazine and the *Mississippi Review*. Shaw's most recent books include *The Night Wages, Cinderbiter, Wolf Milk, Courting the Wild Twin, All Those Barbarians, Wolferland* and his Lorca translations, *Courting the Dawn* (with Stephan Harding).

His essay and conversation with Ai Weiwei on myth and migration were released by the Marciano Art Foundation.

For more on Martin Shaw's work, visit:
cistamystica.com | drmartinshaw.com | schoolofmyth.com

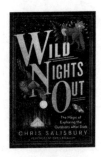

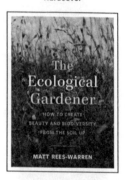